HARRIER!

Into the turbulent Central American republic of Delmira goes journalist John Wolfe. His mission: to find out what a Squadron of RAF Harrier jump-jets is doing in this politically-sensitive area 18 months after Delmira has been granted independence. But he is not the only person interested in the activities and where-abouts of these now-legendary aircraft. Los Enfadados, the Cuban-backed revolutionaries who are stirring up trouble in the neighbouring country of El Libertador, are just as anxious to locate them—but for a very different reason.

HARRIER!

Donald MacKenzie

A Lythway Book

CHIVERS PRESS
BATH

First published 1983
by
Granada Publishing Limited
This Large Print edition published by
Chivers Press
by arrangement with
Granada Publishing Limited
1984

ISBN 0 7451 0019 8

British Library Cataloguing in Publication Data

MacKenzie, Donald
  Harrier!—Large print ed.—(A Lythway book)
  I. Title
  813'.54[F]   PR6063.A243

  ISBN 0–7451–0019–8

The Harrier is a unique aircraft, and not just because of what it can do in the air. It is a high-tech weapon, openly developed in a free country, and produced to military capability under the eyes of the world. In spite of this, its real capability is misunderstood everywhere. What the air forces of the world think they want is jets that will do Mach 2. What they really need, although they apparently don't realize it yet, is the Harrier. Meanwhile we are leading the world.

Air Commodore Sir Thomas Moss,
CBE, DFC, AFC, ADC

HARRIER!

CHAPTER ONE

Acidity burned somewhere in John Wolfe's gullet, reminding him of his last meal. He was weighed down with luggage and equipment, sweating in the street and trying not to seem like a tourist. His was as white a face as any in this black or creole country, and his week in the sun of Mexico City might never have been. Heat wafted down the main street of Delmira City from the overgrown hinterland; spice and perfume hung in the air, tantalizing him with the promise of the tropics. After ten years of freelance journalism it was his first visit to Central America, and what he was most aware of was the acid burning in his gullet.

'You want a taxi, English?' A brown-skinned teenager leaned out from behind the corrugated iron sheet that faced a darkened shop.

'No. I'm OK.'

So he stood out as English. In this place they knew he wasn't an American, and so they would also know he wasn't a tourist. Not many of those in Delmira City, it seemed. Wolfe hefted the leather strap of his tape-recorder, so that it sat more squarely on his shoulder. Walking had made it slip; his skin beneath his shirt was greasing with sweat.

It was the Mexican food that had wreaked

1

havoc on his digestion. Too many chillis, too many jalapeno peppers, and too many ice-cold beers too soon afterwards. And all of them too many times. Mexico had been starting to kill him, and the train journey had all but finished him off. The train had moved slowly down the eastern coast from the capital, then turned south, before the Yucatan peninsula, then into the swamps and nether jungles. All the way, chilli beans and tortillas. Since Mexico there had been two more trains, and two more borders, but he had not eaten since Mexico.

Still the acid burned, making him want to belch.

Delmira City was a one-storey town. It was built on the side of a shallow hill, looking out towards the Caribbean. Everything was made of iron or wood, and anything with paint less than ten years old stood out as if new. Everywhere there were flies, mosquitoes, dogs, black birds of presumably evil intent. The sun came down from the corrugated roof-tops, giving bursts of unpredictable heat in odd concentrations. Shade, wherever it existed, was occupied by squatting people, dressed in bright shirts and trousers, and straw-dropping hats. Children followed him at a distance, holding back after he had barked at one of them outside the station: India had given Wolfe a hatred of beggars, and he had shouted too soon. Delmiran children were not beggars. They were merely friendly, and Wolfe was wondering what he could do to make things up.

He was following directions, because somewhere here there was the hotel he had heard about. It was next to the British Embassy, in a square, surrounded by trees. Anywhere else but the shanty-town of Delmira and Wolfe would have been visualizing it in ideal, Western terms: the Delmira Hilton, perhaps, with fountains on a concourse outside, ice machines on every floor, a coffee shop where you could buy a hamburger twenty-four hours of the day, and a MasterCharge sign discreetly displayed at the reception. But this was the real Delmira, and nothing here gave him that kind of hope.

He had been speaking Spanish in Mexico for more than a week: it was not his best language, but he had started to think in it. He had been prepared for more Spanish here, but was surprised, perhaps pleasantly, to see the preponderance of signs in fractured English. Creole English would be a better description, for that was what he heard jabbering from the transistor radios he heard on every street corner. A legacy of Empire in this case, for until eighteen months before, Delmira had been one of the last remaining outposts of British suzerainty.

Now it was an independent republic within the Commonwealth; the world's newest democracy.

3

Away on the hill, well above the town and all its grubbiness, stood the symbol of that democracy. Parliament House, the only building in the country, probably, built of white marble. Its neo-Victorian bulk, the columns and the steps and the arcade, were like the last cling of Empire. Colonialism was symbolized by buildings like that, but for the Delmirans, of whom there were roughly one million, the intent was liberation from their former masters. The white-and-gold flag flew from Parliament House, as it flew in other more unlikely places about the town, but it was to Wolfe's eyes a half-hearted gesture, as Delmira's own independence seemed half-hearted.

Democracy had been imposed by a Britain anxious to be free of the embarrassments of Empire. Of course, some colonies were still useful, like Gibraltar and Hong Kong, but the problem with Delmira was that it hadn't wanted to let go. At least two Royal Commissions had sat in Delmira, supposedly hearing suits for a separation of the tiny country from its mightily grasping superpower patron, but instead hearing the country's best advocates pleading the case for a continuation of the subject state.

In the end, democracy had been willed, there had been the visit of a minor royal figure, the ceremony of the flags, the beating of the retreat, fireworks and twenty-one gun salutes, the Royal Yacht in Delmira Harbour, and a carnival that was intended to last for a week but which was cut short by the approach of an off-course hurricane. Nobody minded; the royal figure departed, the streets were tidied up, and the majority of the population went back to their normal labour of cutting sugar-cane.

However, Britishness remained. Wolfe saw several fading Union Jack stickers in windows. Traffic drove on the left. Policemen went unarmed, or at least with weapons concealed. There was a Midland Bank, albeit closed, on one of the larger intersections in town. And the signs were in English.

One sign in particular caught Wolfe's eye, and he noted its place for future reference:

ROSTE BEEF AND PUDDING, SPECIAL

Underneath was a photograph of the Queen, its colours bleached to a suitably unpatriotic uniform blue by the daylight in which it was placed. The place was a cheerful-looking restaurant, well attended by crowds of young people. Though none of them, Wolfe could not help noticing, were eating anything remotely like roste beef and pudding.

Thinking he could walk forever in the heat of this city, Wolfe asked directions of a young black.

'Ambassador Hotel?'

'That's by the High Commission, right?'

'Yes.'

'On the way.'

The man tipped his head backwards, indicating the way Wolfe had been walking.

As it turned out he was almost there. A couple of hundred yards further on, and one of the crossing streets was unexpectedly much wider than any of the others. It afforded a sudden view in each direction, left and right. To Wolfe's left he had an almost uninterrupted view of the inner section of Delmira Harbour: a clutter of masts and ropes, a glimpse of silver water, a concrete wall ... but beyond, out in the bay, the low, purposeful lines of a warship. Wolfe's instincts surfaced, and he swung his camera from his shoulder and snapped two photographs almost before he had made the conscious decision to do so. He squinted into the sunlight, trying to identify the ship, but the only flag he could see was limp and pale. It might have been the Royal Navy's Ensign, but equally it might have been a Delmiran flag, or any other.

To his right, the avenue climbed majestically up the shallow gradient towards Parliament House. Here it could be seen that the new building was intended to dominate the town; Wolfe could imagine a time in the future, perhaps when Delmira's political allegiance was less certain than it was now, when infantry would march along this boulevard while a band played, and tanks and armoured troop-carriers and missile launchers crunched the tarmacadam and tramlines, and military men took the salute from the marble building's pillared edifice.

The street was designed on those lines, and as such it was out of touch with the casual, cluttered and careless style of the rest of the city.

Also here was the hotel, fifty yards along on one side: a low building of three storeys, yet one which was larger than many others in the street. To Wolfe's relief it looked modern, or at least recently built, but already it had acquired some of the dusty patina of Delmira City's tropical grime. One window was broken, and had been repaired with card, but aside from that the place was intact and clean-looking.

Beside it was the building the black had referred to as the High Commission. That was how it would always be known to many Delmirans, Wolfe could guess. Yet now its function had been relegated, and the British flag hung from a projecting pole. Wolfe had to pass it to reach the hotel, and he paused for a moment at the bottom of the steps. It looked deceptively accessible: a revolving door to a large hall beyond, and big windows thrown open to the street. But Wolfe knew this casual appearance was carefully contrived: British embassies all over the world were capable of virtually immediate conversion to the status of minor fortress. An armed Marine could be seen in the hall beyond the revolving door, and elsewhere in the embassy compound, away from the street, would be the rest of a small but well-armed garrison. A steel gate would be positioned discreetly beyond the revolving door, and that could be swung into place in a few seconds. Similarly, those wide-open windows had bullet-proof shutters behind them. In any event, the basement of the building would be its real nerve-centre in an emergency.

These were modern times, and diplomacy—the art of creating that which is seemed to be—had taken a new and sophisticated military turn. Preparedness was paramount, even in a place as manifestly friendly to Britain as Delmira.

In his travels, Wolfe had visited British embassies in Europe, the Middle East and the Far East, but none was as casual-seeming as this one in Delmira.

He moved on towards the hotel. As he put his foot on the lowest of the steps leading up to the entrance, something happened that made his heart leap. With an unannounced crashing roar, a jet aircraft shot down the street in the direction of the sea.

Wolfe's instant reaction was to duck, but he recovered his wits in the same moment, and turned quickly to see where the aircraft went.

It was a small fighter. It banked steeply over the harbour, then sped southwards along the coast. Wolfe recognized the outline, and guessed the identity: it was a Harrier GR.3 of RAF Strike Command, the reason for his visit to Delmira, and now, because of its battle-proved status, probably the best strategic warplane in the world.

A group of small boys had seen his reaction to the aircraft, and were laughing and pointing towards him. Nothing surprised them; the roof-top-high passes were made for the benefit of the locals.

Wolfe carried on into the hotel. A few minutes later, as he was checking in and relishing the cool, air-conditioned quietness, a second jet made a low pass over the city. The clerk appeared not to notice.

CHAPTER TWO

BBC Television Studios, Lime Grove, London. The studio lights dimmed while music played, and on the monitors the two men could be seen in silhouette against a pale blue background. The interviewer and his subject stared at each other impassively while, invisible to them, the programme credits were run. The government minister, subject of the live interview that had just gone out, reached forward to take a sip from the warm gin-and-tonic in the water-glass on the table in front of him.

'All right! Off air!' The studio floor-manager stepped forward, signalling with his hands. 'Thank you very much everybody!'

The studio lights changed again, now a more normal illumination. Technicians moved quickly, closing down the cameras and sound equipment. The floor-manager removed his headphones, and went towards the steps leading to the control box. The minister's police bodyguard came forward.

The interviewer stood up at the same time as the minister, and the two men shook hands formally, and rather self-consciously.

'I hope that was what you wanted, Mike,' said the minister.

'Absolutely fine, Charles. Thank you for coming to the studio.' They both made motions with their hands, still awkward in these first seconds off the air: Michael Shelley, the interviewer, collected his notes from the table, and the minister put away the pipe he had not lit all through the twenty-minute interview. The detective was now standing alongside them. 'Have you time for another of those?' Mike Shelley said, indicating the drink.

'If the BBC has any ice.'

'I'm sure we have.'

They turned away and walked across the studio floor, with the detective following.

Shelley said: 'Any chance you can get rid of your goon?'

'He can wait outside.'

Unknown to the vast majority of the two or three million late-night viewers, the two men were old friends. Indeed the minister had only granted the interview because it would be with Shelley. They were the same approximate age, they had known each other in childhood, and although they had been schooled separately, they had been through Oxford together. After that they had gone their separate ways—Shelley into journalism, then television, and the minister into local politics, then Parliament, then government—although socially they remained close.

The hospitality room was on the ground floor, and Shelley had already arranged that it would be supplied with drinks, and that they would not be interrupted. The studio director and programme editor would probably still be in the building when the minister left, to say goodbye and thanks, but for half an hour or so they could relax.

'So how do you feel about it all?' Shelley said when they both had drinks.

'Governmental power, you mean? The same as opposition power.'

'It's not the same at all.'

'Mike, you know as well as I do, the real power in this country lies in the Civil Service. I spend at least half my time trying to combat power struggles in the Ministry.'

'So you say.'

Mike Shelley had hardly seen his friend in the six months since the alliance took office. That

11

had been the thinking behind the interview: the first six months were up, the honeymoon was over, where were the policies?, and so forth. The alliance itself seemed to be holding: ministerial appointments and cabinet posts had been divided up apparently equably, and the two sides in the alliance had managed to keep their peace with their grass-roots parties. Insofar as anything in British politics could be said to be working, the new alliance running the country was working.

But it could not work alone. To maintain its majority in Parliament, it had had to form a second alliance, one of convenience and expedience. The small, demoralized and bitterly left-wing Labour party held the balance of power in the house, and although many of the MPs had sworn they would never vote in support of this centralist government, so far the country had not proved ungovernable under this new and, for Britain, experimental administration. But it could not hold forever, and a new General Election, the second that year, was almost inevitable. It was a risk the alliance was going to have to take.

Some of Mike's questioning in the interview had been on this very subject: when would the PM grasp the political nettle, and consolidate his parties' position? Charles, merely, as he said, the Foreign Secretary, was in no position to say. The timing of a General Election was always the

12

decision of the Prime Minister. True, and Mike knew that very well, but he had pressed his friend on the subject, and, predictably, had been very professionally blocked. No hint had emerged.

But, more surprisingly to Mike, the interview had been blocked on another subject.

He bided his time, wanting to know the truth behind the public silence. He had another drink, and topped up the minister's gin with a little more tonic. Both of them were unwilling to let drink loosen tongues. The hospitality room, party to so many of such post-broadcast confidences, was austere in the BBC fashion, unconducive to either the hospitality it professed or the relaxation it promised.

Shelley knew he could not leave it too late: ministerial duties continued late into each night, and the house was still sitting. He looked for a moment that would allow, then moved in with directness.

'I hope you didn't mind me pressing you on defence,' he said.

'Mind? Why should I mind?'

'You seemed reluctant to talk.' Charles stared back at him. 'You seem it now.'

'You know there are things I can't talk about, Mike. Even off the record.'

'Yes, there are.'

'Defence is one of the things I can't talk about.'

'You didn't answer my question on spending. You ducked it, and I won't be the only person who noticed.'

'I gave you the official answer.'

Shelley put his own drink aside; his head was clearing as if after a sudden shock, and the drink suddenly seemed superfluous. 'And that's not good enough. Not between you and me.'

Charles smiled. 'Why not ask our mutual friend Eric? He's in charge of all that.'

'Because the Cabinet power lies with you, not the Defence Ministry.'

'This isn't Thatcher's Britain, Mike. We don't have a pecking order in the Cabinet. Ask Eric . . . he's in charge of all that.'

Mike sighed. 'Look, Chas, what people are asking, and what *I'm* paid to ask you, is this. If there was another Falklands business this year, or next year, or in the next five years, would we be in a position to do anything about it?'

'We were then.'

'I'm not talking about then. Since then defence spending has stayed level, and we're in hock for Trident. The conventional forces are effectively being run down, that's the case, isn't it?'

'You'll have to wait for the next defence review.'

'I need to be briefed now . . . off the record, of course.'

'There'll be no more task forces, if that's what

you mean.'

Shelley looked at him sharply. 'Now that's an extremely interesting thing to say!'

'That's what it amounts to, doesn't it? If some Third World banana republic picks a fight with us, we want to be able to go in and kick the shit out of them. Or that's what you'd like to see.'

'Is this the new policy?'

'You asked me about spending, not policy. You know where we stand on policy ... we can't decide anything until we get those Labour MPs off our backs.'

'But if there was an election, and it went your way—'

'No comment.' Chas laughed. 'Either give me another drink, or lead me to my car.'

'You're not getting drunk?'

'Of course I'm not. I'm getting talkative, and it's time to quit.'

'This is what I want, so why don't you stay a bit longer?'

Chas squared himself in his seat, and leaned forward.

'All right, Mike. The difference between Margaret Thatcher's war in the Falklands and the present situation is basically political. She had a clear majority in the house, and the Cabinet was either wholly behind her or they knew when to keep their traps shut. You know how different things are now. Anyway, there's no war on, and no sign of one.'

15

'That's what Thatcher and Carrington believed before Argentina moved into Stanley.'

'They were wrong and I'm right. I'm also the Foreign Secretary, and I intend staying in the job. History doesn't repeat.'

'It does, Chas, as you bloody well know.'

'Yes, but not yet it doesn't.'

'All right,' Shelley said. 'The political climate is different. But you can't run down the Navy and Air Force forever without some change made in strategic balance.'

'Our intelligence gathering is much better now.'

'All over the world?'

'All over the parts that matter.'

'You're not telling me anything, Chas.'

'I'm not intending to. You're quite able to draw your own conclusions.'

'So are a lot of people.' The Foreign Secretary's face had gone into the rigid state of non-communication that his political opponents characterized as stubbornness, and Mike Shelley realized nothing more would be forthcoming. At least, not on the general subject of policy. He decided, on the spur of the moment, to try a frontal attack on a specific subject. 'What about the Harrier force, Chas?'

'It's to be maintained.' The face had not shifted; stubbornness or stonewalling, it was much the same. 'Mike, I've got to tell you this. We're old friends, and we're going to stay that

16

way. But for both of us the old days are over. I'm a senior government minister, and there's a limit to what I can leak to you. We're sincerely trying to put right the mess created by the last government, but our political base is too uncertain at present. What we want to do is going to be worth doing, but we can't do it until we've got a firmer base.'

Mike Shelley said: 'The lesson of the Falklands was that there is huge popular support for gung-ho British action.'

'True ... but it wasn't the only lesson, and it's the one that matters least.'

'You're talking about a political base, and what that means is vote-getting.'

'That was Thatcher's mistake. Mike, are you seriously suggesting we should start a war to win a snap election?'

'Of course I'm not. What I'm saying is that the alliance looks more and more as if it lacks the will to fight a war, if one had to be fought.'

'I told you: no more task forces.'

'No more task forces because we lack the *matériel*.'

'I think I had better be going.' Charles stood up, and suddenly it seemed that his dark-suited figure filled the garishly lit room. Mike had been surprised when Charles arrived to see how fit he seemed: he had never been one for exercise, or for any remarkable interest in health, but it had been Mike's experience that politicians in office seemed to age quickly. A congenitally unhealthy and disagreeable way of life, he had always thought. Yet Chas had turned up at the studios half an hour before the broadcast, walking with a spring in his step that had never been there before.

The new alliance was said by its followers to be based on idealism, and for once it seemed that Chas at least was thriving on high office.

The recently appointed Foreign Secretary reached the door, and laid his fingers lightly on the handle. He paused, and looked back.

'Why did you mention the Harriers just now?' he said.

'Because nothing seems to sum up better the British genius for invention, and at the same time the British genius for neglecting that invention.'

Charles grinned back at him. 'My feelings entirely, Mike. You'll be glad to know that we're building up the force as quickly as we can.'

He winked at his old friend, then before anything more could be said he opened the door. The detective was waiting a few paces down the corridor. Mike Shelley stood in the doorway of the hospitality room, watching the two men walking briskly away towards the car park.

CHAPTER THREE

'In our country we have no political prisoners.'

It was said so often it was almost a slogan, and the slogan was repeated so frequently that it had become a joke. In the bars and cantinas the people said it ironically, and in their homes they said it to themselves when the government television told them about their neighbouring countries. It was said because it was true, and it was said because it was not true.

To Luis Guedes, sitting behind the wheel of his transporter, it was a preoccupation.

It was dark where he had brought the immense vehicle to a halt, and silent insofar as the jungle ever was. Yet around him there were shadows that moved, or seemed to, and every sound, magnified by his fear and his uncertainty, was the opening of the stock of a police carbine, or the cautious footfall of one of the Cubanos preparing at last to make him safe.

It amounted to the same thing. There were no prisoners because anyone who was captured was soon made to disappear. And when the Cubanos decided you were a risk to them, they made you safe; when you knew too much, they made you safe; when you knew too little, first they made you unsafe, then in the end they made you safe.

For Luis there was only one subject of

passionate concern, and that was football. Yes, he ravished his wife nightly, and he protected his daughters ... but his son would be a footballer, and the Guedes clan would be famous. In the meantime, he had joined Los Enfadados, the Angry Ones.

He was not angry, no one in his village was angry. But all the men, they had joined Los Enfadados.

It was the Cubanos and their talk of freedom. Who wanted freedom? Who wanted anger? It was always too hot for anger, unless it was a good cause.

That was the mistake the Cubanos made. They spoke of freedom, and how they in their island had made freedom, and they spoke of the junta who ran El Libertador and the gringos who supported them. The land, this land, belonged to the people, and Los Enfadados would fight to restore it.

But it was a mistake.

Life was short, life was hot, life was short of money. It was a bad world if you got interested in it, but it was a good life if you stayed in the bar with your amigos and cheered for the team that was the best in the world. There was food, there was drink, there were women, there was football. The junta you saw on television did nothing to stop the supply of any of those, and what else mattered?

Los Enfadados said that the junta must go.

The Cubanos said that Los Enfadados said these things, and Luis Guedes no longer knew nor cared who said what. For the last three years he had done what he was told, whoever told him. If it was the soldados with their American guns, then he did what he was told. If it was the Cubanos, he did what he was told. If it was the others from Los Enfadados ... well, he did what he was told but he argued always. And if it was Yolanda, he shouted at her and sometimes beat her, but in the end he did what he was told. It was in his nature to flow with the current, to bend with the wind.

Tonight, the Cubanos had told him to drive his transporter to the jungle. Now, five hours later, he was in a part of the country he had never before been to. He was a long way from home, far in the east. Somewhere ahead was the border: maybe the border with Guatemala, maybe that with Delmira. He did not know, because he was doing what he was told.

The Cubanos had left him, telling him to be silent, warning him not to drive away. They had wormed off into the dense black jungle, the five of them like jackals on the hunt. So he sat in the cabin of his transporter, one leg lifted jauntily with his foot against the instruments, declaring he was not concerned. With the same affected indifference, for a while he had swigged back beer from the cans they had left, but the second one had been warm and now both of them were

21

empty. His indifference had been a show no one saw, one he used up too soon. Now he was thirsty again, sweating into his shirt.

Once he had left the transporter cabin, stepped up on to the platform at the rear, and pissed unconcernedly into the jungle foliage crushed beneath the huge wheels. But something had flown past him, and with the screech echoing still he had scuttled back to the comparative safety of the cabin, a dark stain of piss stretching down to his knee.

Outside there were too many enemies: the jungle itself, the Cubanos, the police, the army, the death squads. Los Enfadados were a banned organization, and in this country we have no political prisoners.

What were the Cubanos doing? They had said nothing while he was driving up, except to grunt directions from time to time. The last hour was the slowest, and maps were consulted, away from his eyes. This track, two, maybe three, kilometres long and away from the road, up in the hills, under the thick grey-green foliage of the trees . . . it was near the border, and that must be why. But they would have been more mobile on foot, not in this great transporter.

Luis' nerves steadied after a few minutes, and as the wet stain on his leg started to dry, his head nodded forward and he fell into a light doze.

It lasted no more than a few minutes, because

22

when he opened his eyes again he glanced at his digital watch in the light from the dash. But it had been a long enough snooze to make his neck feel stiff, and to make him impatient and nervy again.

If this was the border with Guatemala, the reason for their trip might be to bring in some men or equipment. There were Cubanos in Guatemala too, and it was common knowledge in Los Enfadados that they worked as one revolutionary army throughout the region. Guatemala or El Libertador were as one country in the worldwide struggle against capitalism.

Luis Guedes, of all the men of Los Enfadados possibly the least committed, had no argument with capitalism. He did not say so to the Cubanos, for that would be unsafe, but he maintained it in his every thought.

Ah, but if this were the border with Delmira, then it was a different matter!

The thought of Delmira stirred Luis' blood as much as did Yolanda in the good times (or Rosaria's glorious *tetas*, when he went to the cantina in the bad times). He, like everyone in El Libertador, everyone, was in no doubt on this subject. Delmira! It strutted its name, its puny flag, as if it were a country! It was a region of El Libertador, a province, a rolling mess of jungle and sugar-cane plantation, and it had no identity. The very name was a challenge to a man like Luis.

While the *ingleses gringos* had been there in their colonial foolishness, Delmira had been an offence to every Libertadorense, but the gringos ruled with the sword and the gun, and El Libertador was a peaceful place. You did not argue with the *ingleses*.

But now the gringos were gone, and Delmira was still there, unjoined with its rightful neighbour, and an insult to all men.

One day soon there would have to be a war with the Delmiran regime; blood would inevitably flow.

But then El Libertador would have an outlet to the Caribbean, and thus to the Atlantic beyond, but to Luis this was a minor matter. Territory and brotherhood came first. It was a question of honour.

He was starting to doze again, and so he did not question why the Cubanos should be interesting themselves in such a principled concern, if this were indeed the Delmiran border. It was hot in the cab, and with the windows closed in a vain attempt to keep the insects out, it was stuffy too. In spite of his discomforts, and the Cubanos' warnings to stay awake, Luis fell asleep, his arms folded across the top of the huge steering-wheel, his forehead resting on his arm.

Then:

'*Hijo de puta!* The son of a whore is asleep!'

Luis was instantly no longer asleep, and he

24

jerked upright. A rifle barrel banged against the windshield and the door was wrenched open.

'You drive! *Bastardo*, you get us to the road!'

With all the commotion of a bad dream, the five Cubanos were all over and around the transporter. They had been in an agitated, dangerous state, as they drove up into the hills, but now they were tired and angry. Luis got the engine started as quickly as he could, but it was not quickly enough for one of the Cubanos, who knocked his hand aside as he primed the diesel engine. The lights came on; then the engine roared, and the two men standing on the rear of the immense machine shouted instructions, confusingly contradicting each other.

Luis, frightened and obedient, bending with the wind, reversed the huge transporter down the track, as the bushes and branches scraped against the steel sides.

He was home just before daybreak, and Yolanda screamed at him for an hour.

CHAPTER FOUR

It took a week for John Wolfe to get accreditation from the British Embassy, and for all of that time he had no choice about what to do. He kicked his heels in and around Delmira City, trying to find some way of putting his

25

idleness to good use, but in general not really succeeding.

He had intended to spend a day at the harbour taking photographs of whatever was there, but in the event he was able to compile a full dossier of shots within the morning. In fact, by lunchtime Wolfe caught himself lining up artistically composed shots of fishing nets and mooring lines, and decided he had done all he could.

Most of that concerned the warship he had seen on his first day, which turned out, disappointingly, to be the flagship of the Delmiran Navy. It was a former British minesweeper of the Coniston Class, built in the early 1950s, and now used by the Delmiran government for coastal patrol duties. Wolfe took a rollful of photographs of the ship, thinking they might come in handy at some time.

The next day he took a bus out of town, up into the hills and to the provincial town (described in the guidebook as 'Delmira's Second City') of San Miguel. The road led past the RAF base, but the bus did not stop and from its crowded interior Wolfe could see hardly anything. The place was barred to him without accreditation, but ironically, because of the preparations he had made earlier in the year, once the bureaucracy had sorted out its paperwork he would have virtually the run of the place.

26

Until then, he was confined to going past in the local bus, and staring through the muddied windows.

San Miguel was not a disappointment. This was because there was nothing there to do or see, and Wolfe had been warned by people at the hotel there was nothing there to do and see. Disappointment breeds only in expectation.

Still, it was a day out of the city, and it gave him a chance to get a glimpse of some of the interior. Geographically speaking, Delmira was a roughly rectangular country, two hundred miles north to south, and about one hundred miles across. Its eastern edge was against the sea. Its western border was in the mountains shared with neighbouring El Libertador.

In the north and east, Delmira was swampy; in the plains around Delmira City the ground had been cleared for the growing of sugar-cane; much of the mountains were still covered by virgin rain-forest. It was in the foothills of these mountains that San Miguel lay.

After a dutiful visit to the Roman Catholic cathedral, and a sweltering walk around the locally prized ruined temple, Wolfe headed for the bus depot and took the next bus back to the capital.

On his third day in town he wrote a short article about his perception of Delmira in its post-colonial state, and telexed it to the nearest office of one of the wire-services. Then for four days he really did have nothing to do, so he caught up on various domestic chores he had been postponing. He had all his clothes laundered or dry-cleaned, he wrote letters to personal friends and sent postcards to relatives, he had his typewriter serviced at the Adler agency in town, he saw every film currently showing in Delmira, visited the one play, watched local television in his hotel room, and, for the first and last time in his life, tasted 'roste beef'. It was *not* special.

Every morning, shortly after nine o'clock, Wolfe walked next door from his hotel to the British Embassy. The Military Attaché was Group-Captain A. L. Lancastar, who always greeted Wolfe in person, was always polite and helpful, but who took eight full days to provide his necessary accreditation. Wolfe never did discover the cause of the delay.

The first time they met, Wolfe asked the Group-Captain what was for him the central question concerning the RAF in Delmira: Why, if British rule was officially ended, were British aircraft with British crews still operational?

'We're here at the request of the government,' Lancastar said. His office was at the front of the building, overlooking the wide boulevard. He had arranged his desk so that both he and his visitors could see down into the street. 'The actual nature of the work we're doing I'll leave you to find out for yourself. You wouldn't take any notice of what I say, anyway.'

'I'm interested in anything you can tell me,' Wolfe said.

'It's better coming from the chaps on the ground, or—'

'In the air?'

'Whichever. I'm just a spokesman these days.'

Wolfe liked the Group-Captain, and during one of their interviews he asked him if he ever flew these days. Just a light plane, was the answer. Back in England. Wolfe had expected, and intended, a piece of reminiscing about the Group-Captain's operational days, but none was forthcoming. He seemed to be in his mid-forties, and very youthful in appearance.

'The RAF is here on a short-term attachment: twenty-four months. The first tour is up later this year.'

'What will happen then?'

'Oh, we'll probably stay on. The deal is indefinitely renewable.'

'The British seem very popular here.'

'We are. Makes a change, doesn't it? Probably the Harriers that do that. The novelty never seems to wear off.'

'Aren't they rather valuable these days?'

'Yes, of course. But they're valuable precisely because of postings like Delmira. We've got no other combat plane that could operate here.'

'Is there any real chance they might ever be

29

used?'

'In anger, you mean?' The Group-Captain's tone was light, at variance with his words. 'As you know, we always work on the basis that combat is likely. That way we're always prepared.'

'The Falklands again?'

'Yes ... and others.' The Group-Captain looked at him shrewdly. 'We never shoot first, but we're always ready for the other chap who takes a pot-shot at us.'

Again the lightness of tone, half-mocking. It was a hint of the old RAF, the one depicted in the movies, the Battle of Britain, the Spitfire, Douglas Bader, and all that. The studied understatement of all things, the schoolboy slang. But Wolfe, who had researched carefully before applying for the visit to Delmira, knew that all that was a thing of the past. The modern RAF was strictly professional, no bandits at nine o'clock, wizard prangs, or any of that sort of thing.

The RAF had its own shorthand, a kind of professional slang, but a strictly workaday one. The language of modern combat flying was sophisticated and complex.

At last, on Wolfe's eighth day in Delmira, the paperwork came through.

When he was admitted to Lancastar's office, another RAF officer was there too. He was introduced as Wing-Commander Wilson-

Brown, and Wolfe was handed a copy of his credentials.

'The Wing-Commander has been instructed to show you everything he can,' Lancastar said. 'You realize that that does not mean *everything?*'

'Yes, of course.'

'Where would you like to start, Mr Wolfe?' said Wilson-Brown.

'Well, could we see the base?'

'Right.' He saluted the Group-Captain, then indicated with his hand that Wolfe should lead the way.

Wolfe nodded to Lancastar, then stepped out into the corridor. Half-leading, half being led, he walked through the Embassy building to where he presumed the car would be waiting. He presumed wrongly. At the back of the Embassy building there was a garden, and beyond this a small courtyard. Squatting on the concrete, like a huge and malignant insect, was a Wessex helicopter.

'I'm afraid you'll have to go in the back,' Wilson-Brown said. 'You've been in one of these before, of course.'

'Yes,' Wolfe said, though he hadn't.

As he scrambled into the equipment bay at the rear, there was a high-pitched whining noise, and the rotors started to turn. After a moment the engine fired, and a bedlam of noise and vibration came through to Wolfe. He could see no way of closing the hatch of the equipment

31

bay, and he panicked momentarily, imagining the helicopter banking steeply over the harbour, with its erstwhile human cargo tumbling arse-over-elbow into the silvery sea . . .

There were several straps attached to the side, and he thankfully slipped his arms through them.

He could see Wilson-Brown, now wearing a white bone-dome helmet, in the left-hand pilot's seat. He was reading over final checks. Beside him, another officer, in flying suit and helmet. Both men were high above him, visible only through a tiny port.

Even craning his neck, he could see nothing past them, and the noise was too great to communicate with them, even by shouting.

Then the whole machine lurched, as if it had tripped over an obstacle in front of it, and amid increasing engine noise it rose from the ground, turning as it did so.

In a few seconds, Wolfe had a vertiginous view over what seemed like the whole of Delmira City, the casual shanty-town arrangement of buildings seemingly submerged in a sea of trees. He remembered seeing not a single tree the whole time he had walked the streets. But this paradox was quickly forgotten as the helicopter swung out across the town, and hastened along the shore, over the harbour and briefly out to sea. Hanging in his straps, Wolfe leaned as far forward as he dared, taking in the view, knowing that the pilot had probably flown this way for his benefit. But it was all moving past too quickly to be taken in. The craft was going lower, and as they re-crossed the coast it was not much higher than the tallest buildings in the city. It was another illusion, but Wolfe had no way of estimating the height.

In no time at all, it seemed, the craft was passing along the perimeter of an airfield. Again, Wolfe craned forward. It had felt, when he passed the RAF base on the bus, that the airfield was placed many miles from the city, but this was right on the edge. Another paradox, this one quickly accounted for. There were no military aircraft in sight. This was Delmira's civilian airport, though to judge by the level of activity, it was not exactly a busy one.

The helicopter circled the airport once, while Wolfe took several photographs. He was not much good at identifying civil aircraft, and all his recent researches had been into the military. But he saw two or three elderly looking dakotas with ambiguous markings, a straight-winged, four-engined aircraft with a high tail and silver-and-blue paint, and several single-engined private aircraft. There was a small terminal building, a tiny control-tower, and about six or seven dilapidated hangars.

After its circuit, the helicopter picked up altitude and turned inland. Soon the city was a long way behind them, while beneath them the

33

greenish, indistinct features of the cane plantations stretched to each side. Occasionally, Wolfe glimpsed teams of people cutting through the cane; a few trucks; several dividing lanes; a warehouse or two.

Then the plantations ended, and wider bush country was beneath. Within a mile or two, Wolfe saw the base.

It was another surprise: it was small and open, possessing only a single runway. As the helicopter descended, Wolfe noticed two camouflaged missile bases on the perimeter, but no one seemed to be around them, then they were passing over the base buildings. Beyond these was a wide apron with three more Wessex helicopters standing in line.

A short way away, standing proudly before the control tower, slightly nose-up in repose, was a Harrier. Two ground-crew were near it, checking off a number of stores from a bogey. Neither of them turned to look as the 'copter settled.

The landing was gentle, such that Wolfe was barely aware that it had happened. He heard the engine-noise diminishing, and felt the craft settle on the wheel-suspension of its undercarriage.

He slipped his arms from the restraining straps, and stood by the open hatchway. After several moments, the pilot and navigator appeared, unhitching their helmets.

Wilson-Brown said to him: 'Why didn't you answer us?'

Wolfe shook his head. 'I couldn't hear you.'

The officer reached past him, and detached a headset from the bulkhead near where Wolfe had strapped himself in.

'Didn't you wear these?'

'No.'

The two men glanced at each other. 'I think there must be some elementary training tomorrow,' Wilson-Brown said.

CHAPTER FIVE

40° 58′ N, 133° 17′ E. 250 kilometres south-east of Vladivostok, the Soviet through-deck carrier *Minsk* was on manoeuvre in the international waters of the Sea of Japan. She was being closely shadowed by ships of the Western Alliance. In particular, elements of the US Seventh Fleet (Western Pacific), as well as a small NATO detachment currently based in Hong Kong. This included HMS *Invincible*, three Type 42 destroyers and a hunter-killer nuclear submarine of the *Swiftsure* Class.

The *Minsk* was being escorted by a total of seventeen smaller warships, including one *Kirov* Class nuclear missile cruiser, three *Sverdlov* Class cruisers and a handful of *Kildin* and *Kanin*

Class destroyers.

Each fleet was watching the other both visually and by radar, and from close-passing aircraft. In the habitual brinkmanship of modern preparedness, each fleet was using the other as a practice enemy. On this occasion, though, extra interest was added by the on-deck activities of the *Minsk*. Steaming into a 14 knot wind, the *Minsk* was exercising her complement of shipboard fighters.

These were the Yakovlev YAK-36MP, code-named *Forger* by NATO authorities. The *Forger* was the only V/STOL combat aircraft available to countries of the Warsaw Pact. So far, three Soviet carriers had been equipped with it.

The advantages of V/STOL for shipboard fighters were obvious, and since 1982 all the major navies of the world had been widening or extending their capability in this area.

The difference between a *Forger* and a Harrier was interesting to Western strategic observers. It was both faster and lighter than a Harrier, for instance, as well as being slightly larger. It was only in those respects, though, that the *Forger* could be said to be superior.

The fundamental design difference between the two aircraft was that the Harrier used a single Rolls-Royce Pegasus engine, with vectored thrust. In other words, the same engine was used for forward flight as for hovering. This enabled the Harrier a flexibility of manoeuvre unique in the world. The *Forger* used three engines: one for forward flight, and two smaller ones for hovering. This introduced problems of synchronization, as well as an inability for vectoring. The *Forger*'s take-offs and landings were slow and cumbersome, since it was incapable of performing rolling take-off.

Perhaps the crucial difference, though, was in terms of armaments performance. The Harrier, fully armed and fuelled, could fly further, could carry more missiles and bombs, and out-manoeuvre anything in the air when it got there. The *Forger*, weighed down with engines and fuel (and the Soviet's traditional dependence on steel-framed aircraft) could carry half the load only three-quarters of the distance, *and* be outflown by the Harrier in air-to-air combat.

Even so, the virtues of Soviet military design—ruggedness and simplicity—together with a fundamentally different approach to aircraft design and tactical profile, made a plane like the *Forger* of great interest to the West.

On this particular day, the *Minsk* had been launching and landing *Forgers* all morning. A variety of conditions were being tried: headwind, crosswind, tailwind, the ship turning, and so on. Once in the air the *Forgers* made a few circuits before returning, but the usual activity in the air around a working fleet continued: ASR 'copters, reconnaissance planes, and Early Warning planes all moved purposefully about.

Just before 1300 hours, disaster struck the *Minsk Forger* squadron. In clear view of the Allied fleet, one of the *Forgers* started to drift uncontrollably sideways, picking up lateral speed as it fell. Shortly before it hit the sea, it started to turn, and the pilot's ejector-seat banged upwards. The parachute opened to break the fall a second or two before the pilot hit the water.

At once, Soviet Air-Sea Rescue helicopters moved in. Signals flashed across the Allied fleet, and two Sea Kings were directed towards the Russian fleet. Only under extraordinary circumstances would they be allowed to approach and offer assistance, but it had become customary for the two opposing fleets at least to go through the motions of offering help when accidents occurred. It was a gesture of marine goodwill, an acknowledgement that the sea was still the common enemy ... and it was the exercise of an excuse to send reconnaissance helicopters in much closer than usual.

By the time the Sea Kings were at their normal point of recall, the Russian pilot had been safely picked up and winched aboard a MIL MI-14 *Haze* helicopter. The Sea Kings turned slowly, and headed back towards their home fleet.

Meanwhile, someone on the bridge of *Invincible* said how tactless it would have been to have sent a Sea Harrier instead.

*   *   *

The capital city of El Libertador was called Prudencia, and it was situated in a wide bay of the Pacific Ocean. The founder of Prudencia had been a sailor, and he chose the site because of its qualities as a natural harbour. It is said that he made his decision on the one day of the year when Prudencia was neither sweltering in humidity nor drowning in torrential rain; certainly he did not live to see Prudencia become a full-scale city. The old part of the city was laid out on lines of old-fashioned grace and spaciousness, with much pretension to culture and political influence.

While walking about the streets of Prudencia, a casual regard of the buildings only might briefly reinforce this pretension today, but the reality of Prudencia's history was turmoil and revolution. A closer regard would reveal bullet-holes in almost every façade; the statuary of Prudencia—commemorating the politically acceptable of the date—was never more than about five years old, anything going further back than that almost invariably torn down in one of the periodic political upheavals.

The most recent of these had been three years before. An extremist faction of the army had staged a coup; three months after they took control, officers of the air force and navy, not to be outdone, had tried to topple the army, and failed. In failing they had managed to express something of the popular feeling of the day, and the result had been an uneasy junta, with generals of all three forces publicly co-operating but privately scheming the overthrow of the other two. Sometimes, though, balance can be found in opposing poles of imbalance, and such was the case in El Libertador.

In fact, this uncomfortable junta had by paradox provided the longest period of stable government in El Libertador since the end of the Second World War, a fact harped on endlessly by the diligent scribes in the junta's press and publicity office.

The junta, like the city in which it resided, was not all it seemed. Both were a façade for something else.

In Prudencia itself, the fraud could be exposed by anyone caring to walk more than a block or two away from the main thoroughfares.

Here the real Prudencia could be found. The streets were narrow and undrained, the houses were derelict and dilapidated, sanitation did not exist, running water was obtainable only in a few places, disease was prevalent and poverty universal. For three decades, people had been migrating to Prudencia from the undeveloped hinterland, falling for the lying claims of successive governments, and seeing at first only

40

the pompous façades of the white-painted town squares.

What they saw second was what virtually all of them only saw last: they gravitated to the squalid back-streets, and from there they never departed.

It was there, less than a mile from the Presidential Palace, that the real, unacknowledged power behind the junta lay. At first sight, the place was no more prepossessing than any other shuttered shop in any other slum quarter of the town. There was no paint on doors or window-frames, and no door or window either. Beyond the entrance was a squalid room, in which, every night, some fifteen local people regularly slept.

At the back of this room was the only feature that distinguished it. There was a second door, leading to the interior, and this had three separate locks. One was fairly straightforward, and would excite no interest from anyone seeing it; the other two were more subtle affairs, requiring a practised measure of pressure and twist to make them operate, and the only clue to their existence was two small holes, apparently hammered at random into the door's edge.

This door was the only way into the interior of the building, a fact which was made certain by an extreme amount of long-term refurbishment that had taken place inside. The walls had been strengthened and soundproofed, all doors had been bricked over and plastered, all windows had been soundproofed and sealed, but in such a way that from outside it seemed merely that dust and debris blocked the light.

The building was regularly de-bugged, and was known to be 'clean'. It had its own generator, and sufficient fuel for six months' continuous running at maximum load. There were emergency food supplies for the entire staff for more than a month. The water-supply was from a well specially dug in the basement, and purified in the building. Air-conditioning ran twenty-four hours a day. There was sleeping accommodation, a games room, a video room, a computer terminal. American newspapers turned up in the building, mysteriously only a few hours after publication. The telephones could be patched in direct to South-Western Bell's network in Texas, by-passing the local system entirely. A telex machine was always maintained, and a telephone in the office of the man who ran the operation was connected direct to Washington. Merely by lifting the receiver, a conversation could instantly commence.

The name of the man who ran this office was Charles D. Platten, from New York City.

Mr Platten was quietly spoken and possessed of restrained manners. He smiled when he spoke; his tone was always reasonable, and he called you by your first name as soon as you were introduced to him.

Mr Platten liked sailing, and he maintained a yacht in Prudencia Harbour. He had a staff of seven: four men and three women. They called him 'sir', and responded instantly to his requests.

Mr Platten was probably something to do with the oil industry.

*   *   *

On the other side of town from Mr Platten's office, the slums were no less degrading or insanitary, but they differed in that they were built against the side of the hills that partially enclosed Prudencia.

In another world or another time, these hills might have provided the background for elegant high-rise apartment blocks, with a superb view of the city and the bay ... but this was the real world, and in it the denizens of Prudencia's neglected streets paid scant attention to scenery. If they thought of it at all it would be as symbolic of the corruption that dominated the Libertadorense regime: all seemed pure, clean and beautiful from a distance, but closer examination revealed the rats.

These southern slums, being physically more remote from the city centre, provided safe refuge for those who opposed the present regime. In some of the squalid streets, men of Los Enfadados were sometimes seen walking

43

openly with their Russian-made rifles slung casually behind their shoulders. But they would only be seen sometimes, and then it would be at night, or when there was a crowded holiday.

Los Enfadados did not yet have the full support of the ordinary people. To gain that they would need first to provide some kind of valid alternative to the junta, for it was undeniable that for good or bad the regime was in control. What public services existed were in the hands of the regime; food was distributed by the soldiers; power was generated by government officials; money was printed by the government. And so on. All Los Enfadados could offer the ordinary people of Prudencia and the rest of El Libertador was the glimpse of a gun-barrel, and the promise that one day that barrel would be pointed into the belly of the three generals. Until then, there was much boasting and threatening, and a certain amount of swaggering.

The men with the rifles were the minority: there were only a few weapons in guerrilla hands in Prudencia, and it was Enfadados policy for these to be seen by the ordinary people as a reminder. But Los Enfadados were not a united organization: the very name was a general one, applied to any group who declared against the regime. Like all other insurgency groups, Los Enfadados were factionalized across a spectrum of opinion, from moderate to extremist. There were Trotskyites, Leninists, Marxists, neo-Marxists, Leninist-Marxists, Maoists; there were concordances with Quaddafi, Arafat and the Red Brigades; some men had been trained in Libya; some had no training at all.

But in the strictly relative terms that are implied by any populist terrorist group, these factions were the intellectual wing.

Behind them were two large groupings. There were those who had a score to settle with the regime. A member of the family might have disappeared, or been tortured, or raped. A death squad might have paid a night-time visit to a certain street. Land might have been seized, or some other important inequity imposed.

Then there were the ones who were threatened, coerced or bullied into membership of Los Enfadados by the Cubans. There were Cuban battalions operating clandestinely all over Latin America, often bringing material relief and assistance to remote villages, or to those dispossessed by the regime, and usually supplying weapons and ammunition. In El Libertador there were thought to be at least three Cuban training camps deep in the mountain rain-forests, where men were trained in the basics of single combat and terrorist warfare.

The Latin American perception of world affairs was fundamentally different from the view taken by the Western Allies and the Soviet

Bloc. The people of Central America considered that the Third World War had already begun, and had been raging since the 1960s. It was a war not between superpowers, but between people's liberation movements and oppressive regimes. It was an undeclared war, but one fought brutally and continuously. It was also a war that could not be fought without superpower involvement.

Each power had its client faction.

On the one hand there were the Western powers attempting to prop up corrupt regimes by massive supplies of armaments and technical know-how; all this on the derelict principle that any regime that declared itself anti-communist must be of essence worth propping up. On the other, the guerrilla, insurgent or liberation forces were supplied by the Soviets, or their intermediary satellites; all *that* on the equally derelict principle that revolution must be continuous.

It was in these ways that military regimes equipped themselves with Exocet missiles and Type 42 destroyers, and why, in the end, the countries of the Third World will be confronting each other with nuclear weapons.

For the moment, though, El Libertador was an interesting case for more conventional reasons. It was a classic case in that there were two warring factions acting as indirect clients to the superpowers, but it was unusual in that both

46

sides had a cause in common.

That was the young independent republic of Delmira. All Libertadorenses were schooled in the assumption that this former British colony was rightfully a part of El Libertador's soil, and the ruling junta knew nothing could unite the country as firmly as a swift military annexation. However, the Argentine cause for Los Islas Malvinas was just as unifying, and the lesson had been learned by association.

In the eyes of the Libertadorense population, this military junta was likely to do many foolish things, but launching an invasion of Delmira was not one of them.

From the Cubans' point of view, based in the slums of Prudencia, the Delmiran question was one that should be played down.

They wanted nothing to distract the hearts and minds of the people from the struggle before them. They did not want the junta to be able to do anything right!

But paradoxically, they were sufficiently sophisticated militarily to realize that if *they* seemed capable of uniting Delmira and El Libertador once more, without the possible humiliation of defeat, then their support on the ground would increase a thousandfold.

However, so far no real method had presented itself.

The field battalion of five men, who had commandeered Luis Guedes' transporter, returned to Prudencia by bus two days after the event. They reported to their battalion commander, were de-briefed, checked for ideological suitability, then returned to one of the training camps.

Their methods of doing something about the Delmiran question might or might not work out, but so far it was the only one there was.

The battalion commander reported to the council, and later in the week the subject was raised again in full session. No one spoke to Havana, because unlike Charles D. Platten of New York City, they did not have a hot line to their base.

CHAPTER SIX

RAF Delmira was very much a fully operational base, constantly on various forms of alert. Everyone John Wolfe met was there for a purpose, and it was abundantly clear that the RAF presence was not just a showing of the flag, the Unit was there to do a job, and twenty-four hours a day were spent doing that job in one form or another. From the moment he arrived, Wolfe was impressed by the professionalism and purposefulness everyone showed, whether it was the pilots themselves, the ground-crew, or even the staff in the tiny canteen and mess. No one considered the Delmira posting a cushy number, even though the facilities in the base itself were superb. It was said that the mess bar was the only RAF bar anywhere in the world with air-conditioning. (That wasn't true, but everyone in Delmira said it to him.)

Every day, Wolfe was either flown or driven to the base from the centre of the city. An officer had been assigned to brief him, and this was Squadron Leader Dave Hartford. Dave—he and Wolfe slipped into first-name terms as soon as they met—was an operational pilot, and certainly did not see his most important function as showing a freelance journalist about the base. As it was, he was exercising every day, and so Wolfe's contacts with him were sporadic.

But at least once a day Dave would settle down for an hour or two's conversation with him, and show him part of the operation, or introduce him to the other pilots.

It was all characteristically easy-going and apparently casual. The air-crew all spoke the technical slang without affectation, or, for that matter, without realizing that much of it was lost on Wolfe.

One day, Dave explained that particular aspect to him:

'The thing is, John, we're flying complex machines under complex orders in a complex world. We're in fast jets, which can bomb or dogfight or attack ground positions, so the machine's versatile to begin with. It carries a lot of different systems: weapons, defence, guidance, radar, computers. We're in contact with the ground and each other. And it's always best that we don't bump into each other or get lost.'

'When you fly a mission, is the aircraft armed?'

'Always.'

Dave's answer came level and emphatic.

'So how do you see the RAF's role here?'

'We're flying warplanes to maintain a state of peace. We're in that job, and it's one which means we defend ourselves at all times, and are prepared to fight if that's what it's all about.'

This led naturally to the topic that was Wolfe's principal interest in Delmira: what the RAF was actually *doing* in the country.

'Well, we're showing the flag,' Dave said. 'Delmira is a member of the Commonwealth, and we're here at their invitation.'

'But you say you're at full combat readiness.'

'There's a border dispute with El Libertador.'

'I know. Is it likely to blow up into anything?'

'Not while we're here.' Dave and he were walking the perimeter of the base while they were talking; it was warm in the sunshine, but a refreshing wind came down from the hills a few miles behind them. On the far side of the airfield, a Harrier was taxiing towards the ski-ramp for take-off. Another routine patrol.

'That's the whole idea.'

'There's surely more to it than that.'

'We have a number of duties here, but that's the main one.'

'What are the others?' Wolfe said.

'Defence of the airport is high on our priorities, and so is air support for coastal shipping. We do a lot of over-sea flying, because reinforcements would come by sea.'

'Reinforcements for what?'

'For us, John. There are only six Harriers here, and although we can fly in and out, with refuelling, it's cheaper to come by sea.'

'Anything else?'

'Air cover for ground forces is part of our brief.'

'You mean the Army's here as well? I didn't know that.'

'I think you should interpret that to mean the Delmiran army.'

'But there isn't one.' Wolfe looked closely at the pilot, but the man merely shrugged. 'Come on, Dave, the British Army isn't here too, is it?'

'I shouldn't have said anything.'

'Is it?'

'Do you want an answer on or off the record?' Dave said.

'On the record.'

'Officially, I don't know.'

'All right . . . off the record.'

Dave glanced at him again, and grinned.

51

'The fact is,' he said, 'I bloody well don't know. They don't tell us anything.'

'So it's just an exercise here.'

'If you like.'

The picture was forming in Wolfe's mind of the military attitude in peacetime. The whole rationale of the military is to fight. But in peacetime, short of starting a war the only thing that can be done is to pretend to have a war. Put like that it sounded futile, but military preparedness amounted to just that: endless practice and exercises, training missions, guns loaded with film and not bullets, missiles fired at dummy targets.

The Harrier on the other side of the airfield pulsed up its engine, rolled slowly towards the ramp, and with an impossible-seeming slowness, climbed into the air. After a few seconds the undercarriage was retracted, and the plane accelerated quickly. In no time at all it was out of sight, low over the distant trees, leaving behind just its echoing roar.

When it had gone, the air-base was deserted of aircraft. The only Harrier remaining was the one Wolfe had been allowed to look at earlier in the day, and that was the one undergoing engine repairs.

Later, when they were back in the coolness of the bar, Wolfe asked the pilot where the other aircraft were.

'You said there were six Harriers based here.

The most I've ever seen together are the two that were here this morning.'

'This is just SMA,' Dave said.

'What does that mean?'

'Squadron Maintenance Area. It's the place we are technically based in, but in practice flight crews and maintenance teams are on constant dispersal.'

'So where are they?'

'Oh . . . all over the place.' Dave's expression was as vague as his answer.

'You mean you're not going to tell me.'

'That's right. The squadron is dispersed throughout the hills. That's why we've got Harriers here, and not, say, Phantoms or Jaguars.'

'But I've often seen four or five Harriers together in the air.'

'We train and patrol in flights. But on the ground we're at dispersal.'

Dave started to describe the thinking behind the strategy, and Wolfe, interested, took notes.

Ever since the Harrier had entered operational service, the flexibility of the machine allowed for a whole new concept of tactical thinking. The Harrier squadrons were mostly in West Germany, literally in the front line of any foreseeable conventional war in Europe. If such a war started, it was certain the first air strikes by Warsaw Pact forces would be against the NATO airfields. Although all airfields were comprehensively defended by surface-to-air missiles, it was certain that most would be knocked out in the first few hours of hostilities, because there never was any practicable defence against a determined attack with nuclear weapons.

Therefore, the British Harriers represented the only likely surviving NATO tactical aircraft after such a pre-emptive strike. This was because the machines and their crews could be dispersed to hide in all sorts of unlikely places.

From these, the planes could be repaired and refuelled, their crews could be rested and fed, and the continuance of air war could be ensured almost indefinitely.

Air-crew were sent to Delmira for regular tours of duty, because there in the tropical forests and hills the whole tactical array of Harrier dispersal could be refined to an art. The danger to Delmira, the Squadron Leader explained to Wolfe, was that the military junta in El Libertador might decide to pursue its territorial claims. In recent years these had been renewed, and El Libertador was into arms-spending in a big way. It was true that the army there was mostly conscript, but the air force presented a huge potential threat, because of its unknown intentions about re-equipping. If a military push came from El Libertador, this base would be high on the priorities for attack. Therefore, the Harriers were dispersed.

'But six craft couldn't fight a war,' Wolfe said. 'It doesn't matter how well dispersed they are.'

'We're preventing war, not fighting it.'

'Even so . . .'

'The British government can't maintain a full garrison in Delmira. But the Harriers could stay undetected and severely hurt the enemy, *if* such a push were tried. But it won't be.'

The six Harriers were a token force, but the Falklands war had revealed how effective a combat aircraft the Harrier was. The opinion of most military strategists was that the Harrier had been the decisive factor in the war.

At least 31 Argentine aircraft had been shot down by Harriers or Sea Harriers. Not a single one of the British aircraft had been lost in air-to-air combat; the nine that were lost were downed in other circumstances. Not even a Harrier can avoid a heat-seeking missile chasing it down the tail.

Although El Libertador's air force was numerically overwhelming, nearly all the aircraft were non-combat, lightweight jets, used as ground-attack counter-insurgency aircraft. The question mark lay on the regime's known plans for up-rating the air force.

'Can I visit one of these dispersal sites?' Wolfe said.

'I'm not sure. They're top secret.'

'I've been given high clearance.'

'I know. I'll have to talk to the Group about that. Anyway, I'm not sure how we'd get you up there. Most of the sites are in places where there are no roads.'

'Couldn't I fly there?'

'If you mean in a Wessex, no. For security reasons no helicopters go up to the sites unless absolutely necessary.'

'Do you have a two-seater Harrier?' said Wolfe.

The Squadron Leader looked at him steadily. 'Do you know how to navigate, Mr Wolfe?'

'No, I don't.'

'We'll teach you a few rudiments.'

Outside on the tarmac, a Harrier landed in a swirl of loose dust. A ground-crew man wearing ear-muffs and white shorts guided the aircraft forward, out of the sun and into the shade of the hangar. Soon the cockpit canopy slid backwards, and inside John Wolfe could see the white-helmeted head of the pilot. A sudden surge of excitement coursed through him, and he knew that whatever obstacles might be put in his way, he would somehow fix himself a flight in a Harrier. He had travelled the world, reported stories of all sorts and from many different kinds of countries . . . but at the age of 33 the sight of this beautiful warplane filled him with a sense of challenge and adventure he had not known since he was an adolescent.

CHAPTER SEVEN

Luis Guedes has spent the early part of the evening at the cantina, where the luscious Rosaria, 18-year-old daughter of his good friend Roberto, had served him several glasses of beer. His thirst had been encouraged by the arrival of each glass, for Rosaria would lean well forward as she placed it before him, and the glimpse he got was a little hint that he should drink up quickly and order another.

Now he was home, and because he was unsteady on his legs, he had fallen across the bed and taken Yolanda with him, against her protests. It was too hot, she had baking to do, it was too early ... but he had undone her and sunk his face in the soft dough of her breasts. That she liked, but when he tried to lift her skirt she had pushed him aside. So he had beaten her, sliding the belt from his trousers and hitting her with the buckle end of it. She screamed, but it was part of what she liked best.

Bruised but not bleeding, she became aroused and lowered her great soft arse on to him, where they both liked it. It was their way of not making little *nenes*, or so they joked, because what they both liked, if for different reasons, was when she slipped her arsehole off him and turned around and sucked him until he came.

He told her it was *asqueroso*, disgusting, but she licked him clean and then perhaps she would lift her skirts again.

Meanwhile, Luis dreamed of Rosaria's teenage *tetas*, and how he would like to remove them from their naughty *camisa*.

But tonight Yolanda was not giving him her tongue. She was down on the bed, face-down and biting the pillow while Luis mounted her from behind, when the door to the village street was kicked repeatedly.

'Ah no,' Yolanda sighed. 'You not stop now!'

Luis grunted and closed his eyes. They could come back later.

But the kicking noise came again and Luis, still *levantar*, still hard-on, stopped his thrusting at her and lay forward across her back, breathing quickly.

'No!' cried Yolanda. 'We go on ... now I suck you!'

'Ssh! I want to listen!'

But now there was silence outside, and in the dark beyond their room Luis could see nothing.

Yolanda tried to wriggle forward and away from him, determined not to be deprived of what she called her *confite*, her candy ... but Luis was still, and pressing her down so she could not move.

'Stay there, woman!'

Luis was staring towards the darkness beyond, because he had heard a noise. Then a man stepped forward, and the light from their bed glinted from the barrel of his rifle.

'Come on, Guedes. You got work to do!'

It was Ramón Mendoza, the one of the Cubanos Luis liked least. He was the one with the violent temper, the easy resort to kicks and threats. It was he who was the self-styled leader of the gang who came to the village from time to time, bringing ammunition for the guns of Los Enfadados, bringing sometimes seed for the fields and fabrics for the women, and dialectic for the meetings. Now he brought a rifle.

Luis started to slide himself from Yolanda's body, but in the instant he felt her muscles clamping around his still erect cock.

'*¡Vate a la mierda!*' Yolanda shouted. 'Fuck off, Mendoza!'

'Hey, Yolanda...' Luis felt a distinct tremor of alarm.

'Shut up, *zorra!* Come on, Guedes. You can have the slut whenever you like!'

On balance more scared of Mendoza than of Yolanda, Luis slid back from her. His cock was starting to lose its erectness anyway. Yolanda swore at him as he pulled free, but she lay still on the bed, presumably keeping her bared breasts from Mendoza's eyes. The Cubano, noting from which part of her Luis had pulled himself, nodded.

'We'll come back soon. She will wait for you.'

'*¡A hacer puñetas!*' Yolanda swore again.

59

'Hey, Mendoza, she is my wife.'

'Only a slut takes it in the arse.'

Luis scowled, but he had made his stand against the Cubano, and was scared to go further. Yolanda started to raise herself from the bed, but Mendoza smiled, and so she turned her head away angrily. Luis pulled on his trousers, slid the belt into the loops, stuffed his shirt inside. Yolanda, now abandoned by him, reached back angrily to tweak down her skirt over her exposed backside.

'Yes, you cover it, *puta!*' Mendoza said. 'Or I'll pleasure you myself.'

Luis scowled at him, but Yolanda, pushed beyond submission, rolled off the bed and stood uncaringly before the two men, her great animal breasts swinging free. Luis saw the two dark-brown nipples, the size of small saucers, where he had so often nuzzled happily. She snatched a shawl, folded it quickly over her shoulders, half covering her *melones*.

She snatched up a bottle by the neck, and advanced on the Cubano.

Luis stepped forward quickly, and grabbed her wrist.

'No, Yolanda!'

'I'll kill him!'

But Luis, although frequently intimidated by her rages, was accustomed to grappling physically with her. He bent her wrist back, and the bottle bounced away unbroken across the wooden floor.

Mendoza had watched all this unperturbed. He signalled roughly with the barrel of his rifle.

'Come, Guedes! No more time.'

Yolanda had turned away, and from the way in which her shoulders were moving Luis sensed that she would soon explode with uncontrollable anger.

He crossed quickly to the door, and the two men went out into the darkened village street.

It had all happened so quickly that Luis could still feel his cock large in his pants. He was physically unsatisfied. He could smell the fragrance of Yolanda's *cono* on his hands, and that gave him a wish for more.

'Lucky bastard, eh?' said Mendoza.

'Shut up.' As he said it he felt he was throwing away his life, but the short incident had obviously amused the Cubano. He put his arm briefly around Luis' shoulders.

'You can screw her later. Now we got work for Los Enfadados.'

'I'd rather be screwing.'

'Wouldn't we all? But you won't be unhappy where we're going.'

'Where are we going?'

But Mendoza said no more, relapsing to his more usual taciturn shelf.

They had walked only as far as the end of the village when Luis was no longer in any doubt at all. They were going to the yard where the

61

transporter was parked.

'No! I got into trouble last time! They said I lose my job if the transporter is stolen again.'

'We need it.'

The padlocked gate of the yard had already been blown open, and the gates swung back. The lock had vanished; Luis could not remember hearing a shot, so perhaps this time they had smashed their way in with crowbars.

Two of the Cubanos were standing on the platform at the rear, their rifles held in their hands. The remaining two were sitting in the dust by one of the great wheels, but they were all on their guard, because as soon as Luis and Mendoza appeared they leapt to their feet, holding their rifles in a businesslike way.

'It's all loaded,' said one of them.

'And the girl?'

He cocked his head towards the cab.

'Good,' Mendoza said. He turned to Luis. 'We need fuel . . . you fill her up.'

'If I do, I never work again.'

'Your choice, Guedes,' Mendoza said. He made no threatening move or word, but Luis could somehow tell by the icy voice that there was, in fact, no choice.

'Okay.' He went around to the left side, legged up, gripping the sides of the cab, and clambered into the driver's seat. He was now some three metres above the ground, so huge was the transporter.

Someone was already there, crouched frightened against the back of the seat, and Luis looked at her in surprise.

'Rosaria!'

'Are you one of these?' she said, and he saw in the dim light from the dash that she had a red streak, like an incipient bruise, over one eye. Her hair was awry, and her eyes were frightened.

'You know who I am. Why are you here?'

'They made me come. Where are we going?'

'I don't know.'

Mendoza had climbed up into the cab while they spoke, followed by the man they had talked to outside, Miguel. Luis primed the engine with automatic movements, eyeing the frightened Rosaria as he did so. She was wearing the clothes he had seen her in earlier: the white, low-cut blouse and the blue skirt with the frill and the coloured flowers, but the jauntiness was gone from her. In the cantina she carried the flirting and backside patting with flair and indifference, using her youthful body to earn herself tips but not trouble. Every man in the village dreamed of fucking Rosaria, but not one of them would dare try.

But such was her cowed state now that Luis wondered, letting the thought flicker across his mind, if she had been raped.

The engine fired, and Mendoza settled himself in the right-hand seat, forcing Rosaria to

63

move away from him and towards Luis.

Luis rapped the dash, checking the reading of the fuel-gauge. He let up the clutch, and slowly wheeled the great articulated vehicle round, heading for the fuel-pump.

Here he had to clamber down again, and while he pumped more diesel fuel into the tank one of the Cubanos riding on the back stared down at him.

No weapon appeared, but Luis was in no doubt that if he tried to run, or to do anything other than what they told him, he would be shot.

Not knowing what was wanted, but suspecting that they were returning to the mountains, Luis filled the tank to the top. It almost depleted the yard's supply of fuel, but he was philosophical about that. He knew that when he returned there would be no more driving job for him.

'All right, where do you want me to take you?' he said, when he was back at the wheel and had the engine going again.

Mendoza nodded his head forward, signifying straight on beyond the gates, which Luis interpreted to mean they were going back to that mysterious place in the mountains. Outside the village, about eight kilometres on, they reached the one stretch of divided highway in the region, and Luis took the great lumbering vehicle up through the gears, knowing that there would be no other chance for that comparative luxury once they reached the rougher tracks of the foothills.

It was at least two hours before midnight— Luis had taken off his watch while screwing Yolanda, and in his haste had left it behind— and the air on the plain was as usual warm and humid. He drove with the window open, while on the far side of the cab Miguel too had his wide open, and so air blustered around them.

Rosaria, beside him, was careful not to lean against him, and if the vehicle ever lurched to the side, pressing them together, she was careful to separate them afterwards.

On her right, Mendoza made no effort to stop himself falling against her, but from time to time she pushed him away.

Luis was ever-aware of his close glimpse of her well-formed breasts, poking roundly over the cut of her blouse. Yet tonight he felt protective of her, he wanted to keep these bears away from her. She was the daughter of his friend, a child of the village.

Even so, when the curve of the road pressed her shoulder against him, he felt the strip of warmth where they touched as if it were a heated electric element.

No one in the cab spoke, so after a while the rhythm of driving lulled a sense of contemplation into Luis's mind, and he began to think of the reality of what might happen to him on his return to the village.

Perhaps he would not lose his job after all. On the last occasion the Cubanos made him drive the transporter, he had been reprimanded and warned, but he had not after all been sacked. He was proud of his driving ability, of the strength that was needed to take this great lumbering machine along the rough tracks around the quarries and workings, and he knew that drivers like him were hard to find or train. Sure, they had threatened to bring in a man from Prudencia to replace him, but after all they had not.

In the countryside, it was indeed Los Enfadados and the Cubanos who ran things, just as Mendoza once had said.

In Prudencia there was always the *policia* to back up the rulings of the junta, but out here there was no one. Just the Cubanos.

Ramón Mendoza was now his friend, was that not so? If he was threatened with the loss of his job, he could call on Mendoza.

Reassured by his own reasoning, Luis ceased to worry about the consequences of this unwitting expedition. Gradually his mind turned to the other great preoccupation of the moment.

He could still feel his desire throbbing away in his loins. For that he cursed Mendoza. It was always the same, if he finished without finishing. He urgently needed a fuck, a release of the excitement he now held back.

And beside him, the child Rosaria with the woman's body. More and more often, he stole a sideways glance at her breasts, fantasizing about their weight in his hand, their nipples playing across his lips. Why was she here? To torment him? Had Mendoza brought her for the pleasure of them all? Or was there some other reason, not related to Luis' own suppressed desires?

They reached at last the end of the divided highway, and at once the standard of the road deteriorated. The vehicle was forced to slow, to move down through the grinding gears, and as they started the series of long climbing turns, through the roads of the hills, the cab bucked and swayed, and many times Rosaria was thrown against the two men on either side of her. Soon, even Luis ceased to notice.

Higher and higher they climbed, and the air cooled. Rosaria said she was cold, that she wanted something more to wear, but Mendoza told her to shut up. Luis wound up his window. Eventually, so too did Miguel. It became much quieter inside the cab; warmer too.

Mendoza was now very much in control, directing Luis as he had done before, apparently knowing his way through these night-clad hills without benefit of a map. They were soon a long way from anything that could be described as a made-up road, and as Luis manoeuvred the great vehicle along the tracks, he could hear the bulk of the hydraulic crane on the platform behind tearing and scraping through the overhead branches.

At last Mendoza directed him to stop. He and Miguel climbed out, and Luis could hear a conference going on above and behind him. He looked at Rosaria, and she looked at him. She seemed frightened still, and he seemed unable to console her. Moments later, the two Cubanos returned to the cab, and Mendoza directed him onwards. There was not much further to go.

A few minutes later, Mendoza told him to halt, and Luis switched off the engine. The silence that followed seemed immense.

'Okay, Guedes,' Mendoza said. 'You wait here. You do not drive away, you do not leave the cab. If you see or hear anything, you do nothing and keep still and quiet. The only time you do *anything* is when I tell you. You got that?'

Luis confirmed that he had. 'How long am I going to wait?'

'Until we get back.'

'How long will that be?'

'One hour, ten hours, two days. Who knows?'

'But—'

'There's some food behind you. And water. You can get out to take it . . . but otherwise, you stay in here.'

Rosaria said: 'What about me?'

'You stay here too.'

68

Mendoza and the other man climbed down, and once again Luis and Rosaria glanced at each other in the dim glow from the dash. They heard Mendoza walking around the front of the cab.

'Hey, Luis!'

Luis opened the cab door, and bent downwards to where Mendoza was now standing.

'She is for you,' Mendoza said. His voice was almost a whisper.

'But, why . . .?'

'We like you. You are useful. Later, you'll do what we tell you.'

Before Luis could say anything, the man had hefted the rifle on to his shoulder and moved back into the dark. Luis straightened, then slammed the cab door. From the jungle Mendoza's voice called: 'Kill the lights!'

Luis complied, and the darkness and silence was total.

Then Rosaria said, very quietly: 'If you touch me, I'll scratch you to pieces.'

'Okay, I wasn't going to . . .'

'I'm cold and I'm tired. I'm going to sleep, but you must not so much as move.'

'Okay, okay.'

He heard her move in the dark, fabric rustled, then something touched his leg. It was her head.

She said: 'Don't you dare touch me!'

'But—'

'I need a pillow.'

There was a long silence, while Rosaria lay stretched across the cab's hard seats, with her head resting on Luis' thigh.

Then she said: 'I'm cold. Put an arm around me.'

He had been scared to move, but now he laid an arm around her, blundering in the dark and resting his forearm on something of her that was soft. He realized instantly that it must be one of her breasts, but he was too scared to move away. She pulled his arm comfortably against her, and he heard her make a pleasure noise.

He felt himself hardening. Again he dared not move, but now Rosaria kept shifting slightly, and he felt the soft swelling move gently against his arm. Very slowly, so as not to rouse her anger, Luis brought his other hand over to her, moved it sensuously over the soft swelling of her chest, felt the line of her blouse, and paused. Rosaria made no move. Luis' heart was pounding, and the tightness of his cock, pressed between his thighs, increased so that he thought he would burst.

With a caution and gentleness Yolanda would not have recognized in him, Luis moved his hand down, slipping it beneath the light fabric of her blouse. She wore no constraining *sostén*, a fact he had always guessed from the fluidity of her movements in the cantina, and a fact he now rejoiced in, feeling the freedom of her breasts.

70

Rosaria groaned. His hand took the full round weight of her breast, and the soft little pea of her nipple moved coyly under his stroking fingertips.

But then she abruptly moved, lifting her head and raising her body so that his hand could no longer feel. Reluctantly he let his hand slip from her blouse. He froze, thinking he had gone too far too quickly.

She spoke, though, and her voice was thick with suppressed desire.

'I want what you want,' she said.

Her fingers were at the clasp of his trousers, and then he felt a light touch on his cock, a quick release from its constraint, and warm breath moving over the sensitive skin. Her lips took him at once, and she sucked and sucked, her face buried in his lap.

When he had come to climax, his breath rasping over the nighttime noises of the mountain forest, she rested against him with her mouth still loose and moist around his cock. Then they both fell asleep.

CHAPTER EIGHT

Charles D. Platten, of New York City, was sailing in his private yacht, *Saigon*, in the wide bay that fronted the city of Prudencia. It was a hot, blue afternoon, with a number of the white-painted yachts of the wealthy plying to and fro around the harbour. To the east, the white high-rise buildings of the new downtown section glittered in the sunlight.

Mr Platten never sailed alone, for he was of a nervous disposition, and although he had a sound Navy background he had never learned to swim. His staff from the Prudencia office took it in turns to accompany him when he went sailing, one of the prerequisites of their appointment to his office being that they were proficient in the skills of life-saving.

Today, his crew was one of the multilingual secretaries, a young woman, originally from Casper, Wyoming, but latterly from Washington DC, called Mary-Ellen Walen. Mary-Ellen, conforming to Mr Platten's stated preferences, went topless on his yacht, sunbathing prominently on the foredeck. Because she had been in Prudencia for more than a year, Mary-Ellen had acquired a deep and beautiful suntan, one that covered her body uniformly. This was because one of Mr Platten's other stated preferences was that as soon as the *Saigon* was a respectable distance from the shore, and thus beyond the range of even the most powerful binoculars, his accompanying staff should also remove the bottom half of their costume. They continued to sunbathe on the foredeck, however, as it was part of Mr Platten's scheme that passing yachts should be in no doubt of what was going on aboard his ship.

What was going on aboard his ship was precisely what appeared to be going on: nothing beyond what could be seen. Mr Platten cruised for pleasure and relaxation.

His crew, however, cruised as a part of her job (it was always one of the female members of staff). Whether or not Mr Platten liked to look at naked female breasts and genitals had never been finally established by anyone, but what was certain was that he never made the least move to take advantage of the women.

Mr Platten, it was generally agreed by the staff in their rare moments of confidence off-duty, was probably asexual.

What they did not discuss, because they knew better, was that the *Saigon* was equipped with transmitting and receiving radio equipment of a sophistication you would not normally expect to find on a yacht of her size. Although Mr Platten cruised for pleasure, there always came a moment during his voyage when he went below deck for several minutes, and for that time he was certainly not at leisure.

Today's voyage had been entirely typical, and now Mr Platten and Mary-Ellen were returning slowly to Prudencia, Mr Platten's radio conversation being some half an hour behind them. They were approaching the moment in the voyage where Mary-Ellen, by long experience, was about to don the bottom half of her bikini, thus removing her genitals from the view of Mr Platten in particular and the Central American republic of El Libertador in general.

Her breasts would be removed from the same views only after docking in Prudencia's harbour.

The tranquillity of the afternoon was abruptly broken by the sudden appearance of a small jet aircraft. It was moving along the distant coast to the north, then swung suddenly out to sea. It turned again, and headed in the general direction of Mr Platten's yacht.

'Miss Walen, you should watch this,' said Mr Platten, and Miss Walen sat up and looked in the direction of the noise.

She recognized the jet immediately, as she was trained to do, as a Cessna A–37B of the El Libertador Air Force. The plane dipped its nose, moved closer to the surface of the sea, and flew past them only about a hundred yards away. Both Mr Platten and Mary-Ellen turned to watch its progress, as the noise from the plane's twin engines seemed to rock the boat.

There was a sudden burst of gunfire, a huge white cloud of spray shot up in the distance, and the plane banked away.

'What are they aiming at?' cried Mary-Ellen.

'Target practice, I think, Miss Walen.'

The jet was now out at sea, banking again. As the cloud of spray subsided, it could be seen that a small motor-boat had been the intended target. It too had turned, and was making for land at top speed. Two men were visible on the deck, crouching low; one of them was pointing at the jet aircraft, which was quite evidently in the middle of making a wide turn to make a second pass.

A third man appeared on deck, and he was carrying two weapons. As the jet came in, he and one of the men took aim and opened fire. The boat started taking evasive action.

Mary-Ellen, in her excitement, stood up for a better view.

The jet came in, lower than before, and once again passed Mr Platten's yacht.

'*Go-go-go-go-go-go!*' Mr Platten was shouting, waving his fist in a circular motion.

The jet opened fire, and white spray spat upwards from the sea once more. The two men on deck vanished, as if blown away, and the speeding motor-boat veered to one side. As the spray settled and the jet screamed away, the boat could be seen roaring around in a tight, uncontrolled circle.

Mr Platten returned to the helm of his yacht, and steered her well away from the crippled boat. Meanwhile, the plane was circling again. This time its approach was higher, and it seemed to be flying more slowly. As it passed over Mr Platten's yacht, a large black cylinder fell from beneath one of its wings, and tumbled seawards with an apparently leisurely end-over-end motion. It fell into the tight circle described by the speeding motor-boat.

An immense explosion came next, throwing up a sudden mountain of white spray and orange flame, with the fragments of the boat hurled outwards. The sound hit Mr Platten's yacht about a second later, and it and the blast-wave, although diminished by distance, almost dislodged Mary-Ellen from her precarious position. She shrieked, and grabbed at one of the ropes, steadying herself as a quarter-mile away the mound of water and debris collapsed back into the sea. Mr Platten's fist was still clenched, and his eyes were bright with excitement.

'Hooo-eeh!' he yelled, and the veins stood out on the side of his reddish neck. 'Right smack in the middle!'

All that was now left of the motor-boat was a cloud of smoke drifting away seawards, and a few fragments of wood and rope, fleetingly visible on the swell of the ocean. The A-37B had returned northwards, whence it had come.

Peace and tranquillity were sifting back.

Mr Platten steered the yacht towards Prudencia harbour.

'You may resume sunbathing, Miss Walen,' he said. 'And would you please put your drawers on again?'

Mary-Ellen complied, then lay back peacefully on the foredeck, as the *Saigon* nosed quietly towards her berth.

* * *

It having been agreed that John Wolfe could travel as a rear-seat passenger in a Harrier during a training flight, his elementary 'training' was under way. It made his head spin, as it gave him a glimpse of the immense amount of real training fast-jet pilots had to receive. Some of his preparations were mental, some physical.

His life had made his body soft, and fitness was essential. Every day he did what the RAF called 'aerobics' with the pilots based at the SMA. Until this, he had had no idea how out of condition he had been getting. There wasn't much difference that could be made in a few days, but there was some.

His teeth were examined by a RAF dentist, and some of his fillings replaced. He was told not to eat flatus-making foods before a flight. 'If the machine suddenly decompresses, your fillings will burst out, and if you've been eating beans your stomach might explode.'

He drew a g-suit and a bone-dome from stores, and got used to putting them on. The bone-dome was tailored to fit his head exactly, so that when putting it on he felt as if his ears folded painfully flat against his head.

CAP = Combat Air Patrol. FRCs = Flight Reference Cards. CBU = Cluster Bomb Unit. Pipper = the aiming dot in the gun-sight. ATC = Air Traffic Control. EW = Electronic Warfare.

'You've got a high security rating, but I must ask you, Mr Wolfe, to kindly sign this copy of the Official Secrets Act.'

'In the cockpit you must have your belts as tight as you can bear. A Harrier moves about the sky in a way that is entirely its own. It isn't going to go where you expect it to.'

'We use the ski-jump for take-off, to get the maximum load aboard, but because we fly to dispersal we go for RVL. We try to burn as little fuel as possible. It's cheaper, but it maximizes our operating range.'

RVL = Rolling Vertical Landing. SOP = Standard Operating Procedure. ECM = Electronic Counter Measures. PBF = Pilot Briefing Facility. SAP = Simulated Attack Profile. SAM = Surface-to-Air Missile. AOA = Angle of Attack. IFF = Identification, Friend or Foe.

'The best thing about a Harrier is its flexibility. It can be used for ground-attack, air-to-air combat, anti-submarine warfare, and it can carry bombs, rockets, air-to-air missiles, cannon. On training missions, like the one you'll be on, we carry armed weapons, but we fire only film.'

'What you'll be riding in is the supreme achievement of the British warplane industry. There's only one thing wrong with a Harrier, and that is that we sold the idea to the bloody Americans. They have a variant called the AV–8A, and it's used by the Marines. The Marines like it. But from the American point of view, a Harrier is a "foreign" aircraft; it's almost unprecedented that the Pentagon should buy a "foreign" aircraft for use by its own forces. Tough political pressure, so the plane was Americanized, and through lousy government decisions in Britain, all future development of the plane is to take place in America. The kickback is that Britain is still a manufacturer of major parts, such as the engines. But lately the Pentagon hasn't been able to decide whether or not to go on with production.'

'It was an American who invented viffing. Vectoring in forward flight. We give them that, they came up with something. What it means is that a Harrier is able to slow down sharply and suddenly in level flight. Best thing you can do if there's an enemy following you! He skids by underneath and you squirt off a Sidewinder at him, and that's the end of him. The only plane that can outmanoeuvre a Harrier is another Harrier. And then only just.'

'A new Harrier costs about £15,000,000. We don't like losing them, but not only for that reason. Every one we lose is one less that we have. The new generation of Harriers, if the Americans go ahead with them, will be bigger and better. Probably have air-conditioning, too.'

'If tactical war breaks out in Europe, and it doesn't go nuclear straight away, the only NATO warplane in the skies after the first day will be the Harrier. No F–16s, no Jaguars, no Phantoms, no Mirages. Just the Harrier, flying from fully operational dispersal sites.'

Squawk = Radar Identification Signal.

Recover = Return to base.

Gotcha = Sudden snatch raid on air-crew recovering to base. The most unpopular form of survival training ever devised.

Clangers = Cockpit Warning Signals.

Bogie = Enemy Aircraft.

Bunt = A dive. To dive.

Ninety = 90° turn.

Wanker = Wanker.

*   *   *

The following day passed slowly and, within

certain definitions, pleasurably for Luis Guedes.

The temperature in the transporter's cab started to rise soon after dawn, and by mid-morning it was humid and airless in the forest. He and Rosaria were soon soaked in sweat, even though they kept doors and windows open to try to encourage a through draught. Luis removed his shirt, and tried to persuade Rosaria to do the same, but she would have none of it.

'You think I am wicked girl.'

'No I don't,' he said, but he was lying as well as telling the truth.

'Never! Never do I do such things!'

But as the day passed, and it became abundantly clear that neither of them had anything to do or anything to talk about, the likelihood of her never doing such things diminished. Damp with sweat, her little blouse stuck maddeningly to her *tetas*, and later in the day, when Luis discovered that the Cubanos had loaded a huge water-tank on to the back of the transporter, he and the girl were able to wash. When her turn came, Rosaria unself-consciously stripped off her clothes and washed herself down. Then she dressed and became inviolable again.

Luis tried to keep his mind off her.

But then, what was there for him to keep his mind on? Birds flew around above them, but mostly they were invisible in the foliage. Animals and birds called endlessly, but they too

81

were invisible in the trees. For a while something rather large slithered around noisily near the wheels of the transporter, but neither he nor the girl cared to climb down to find out what it might be.

Of the Cubanos, there was no sign at all.

In the early afternoon, things briefly became interesting again.

Rosaria said: 'Come, I suck you again.'

Surprised, Luis said: 'Hey? You mean—?'

'You like it again?'

She reached for his trousers and pulled them open, and with expert fingers whipped out his cock. It lay softly in her palm. She bent to her kissing of it, but after two minutes it was as limp as ever. Luis frowned, and tried to think about Yolanda's arse-hole, but nothing came of it. What a reverse! Three days ago he would have thought, with Yolanda, of Rosaria's breathless lips upon him. He reached beneath as he had done before, feeling for that elemental softness of her breasts.

But Rosaria had tired of his lack of response, and she moved back from him. 'You tired, Luis?'

'No . . . it was you started too quickly—'

'Poot!'

She affected a lack of interest, and stared away from him through the open door. Half a minute later, Luis had an erection like a long loaf. 'See, Rosaria?' She glanced back at him, then turned away again.

There was no restoring her interest. A few minutes later, Luis clambered down from the cab and walked around the huge transporter, professionally making a check of the hydraulic equipment and the tyres. The load-platform at the rear was fourteen metres long, and the transporter could lift and then carry a load of nearly 6,000 kilograms. It was certainly the only one of its kind in El Libertador, and probably one of only a few in all Central America. Luis, in spite of his many other failings, was proud of his work and very good at it. He loved his great truck, and his life was made worth living by his use of it.

Satisfied that no damage had been done to the transporter during the drive up, and that the Cubanos had not vandalized it, Luis took a chunk of bread and a piece of cheese from the provisions the Cubanos had left. He filled a bottle with water, then climbed up to the cab.

Rosaria was waiting for him. She was leaning back against the opposite door, one foot up on the seats. She had roughed through her hair, and drawn the front of her blouse lower than before.

'You still want me?' she said.

Luis, chewing bread and cheese, said: 'Sure.'

He swallowed water while Rosaria stripped off all her clothes. As she crawled across him she said: 'Anything you like . . . but no fuck, okay?'

'*No fuck!*' He gestured impatiently. 'Then what you doing to me?'

'I am still *virgen*,' she said, playing with the clasp of his trousers. 'I am staying *virgen*, so no fuck.'

After that she did not say very much more.

Luis and Rosaria were left, undisturbed, in the transporter for one more night, and half the following day. At the end of it all, Rosaria was still *virgen*, and Luis was fairly tired.

CHAPTER NINE

Suddenly it was going to happen. Standing next to the two-seat Harrier, waiting for the word to go, Wolfe felt dwarfed and intimidated by its size. All the time he had been at the SMA he had seen Harriers regularly moving about the field, and sometimes he had been quite close to them, but this was the first time he had been right up beside one. He was so close to it that he could see past the dark air intake to the impeller blades of the engine compressor. The plane stood high above him, seeming much larger than it should ever be.

What impressed him most, the single thing, was the overall professionalism of the RAF. They had taken his intrusion into their ordered lives completely in their stride; his request for a flight in a Harrier—which he had made simply so that he could later say he had asked and been turned down—had been taken seriously, and since then they had moved quickly and purposefully towards making it possible.

And now, on the spot and waiting to go, Wolfe was still daunted by the brisk yet apparently casual preparations for their flight.

Meanwhile, he had a hollow feeling in his gut and his legs felt weak. Thoroughly excited by the prospect of the flight, he was nevertheless scared witless by the same thought.

His pilot was going to be Squadron Leader Dave Hartford, the same man who had earlier briefed him on the RAF's job in Delmira.

Wolfe could not claim to have grown to know Dave, impeccably friendly as he had proved to be. After several days of worrying about it, Wolfe had come to the conclusion that the cause of it was the essentially one-sided nature of their relationship. Dave had simply pumped information and facts at him, always in a cheerful, slangy and apparently opinionated way ... but there had never been anything for Wolfe to give back. No anecdotes from his own past life had any bearing on that of a Harrier pilot posted to Delmira, and thoroughly absorbed in his flying. Nor could he hold any opinions on any matter that would be relevant to him, nor could he offer any advice or help or even jokes.

It was as if the pilots, young and healthy and totally dedicated, had expanded to fill the world they now occupied, so that they were never defensive about it, never profoundly questioned any aspect of it, never needed any input or stimulus from outside to be able to do their job.

And to cope with the tremendous technical skills necessary, and, doubtless, with the consequences of what they were trained to do, their inner personalities were concealed behind this façade of skill, professionalism, camaraderie and enthusiasm. All of which, John Wolfe never for one moment doubted, was sincere. What it meant, he supposed, was that a combination of the initial wish to become a fighter pilot, and the rigorous and lengthy training they underwent to achieve that ambition, produced a highly specialized human being.

Often Wolfe had envied the pilots their sense of comradeship, and he had felt excluded from their circle, simply by the lack of his own background.

Also, shockingly, they made him feel his age. Until this trip to Delmira he had never considered that being 33 was old. But the flyers were all in their twenties, and most of them were in their early twenties.

Dave Hartford appeared.

'All right, John, if you're ready we can take off.'

Casually said, but momentous.

'Yes, I'm ready,' Wolfe said, and one of his kneecaps started trembling inside his g-suit.

Ground-crew were moving around them, and with the help of one of them Wolfe climbed the ladder leading up to the rear seat. AIRCRAFT ARMED, it shouted in red and yellow on a fluttering notice. He glanced back, saw the canister of Matra 68mm rockets, obviously deadly and live. He turned back to the climb, closing his mind to where he was and what the machine was built to do.

He had rehearsed getting into the cockpit in a mock-up in one of the HASes (hardened aircraft shelters) on the base, but somehow it had not prepared him for the reality. The real cockpit made him feel large and clumsy: it seemed there was no room for a man inside, but he got first one leg and then the other down, sliding them past the seat and down into the depths of the fuselage beneath the instrument panel, lowering his backside on to the barely padded navigator's seat. Then he was shifting and easing his body, trying to make it fit snugly into the too-small area.

In front of him, and lower than him, Hartford was similarly easing himself into place. *Once we're in the cockpit*, Dave had said to him the evening before, *you'll be too busy to be worried*. He had not believed it then, but now it was true. A member of the ground-crew was standing on the ladder, looming over him, and reaching down into the cockpit to help connect him into the vitals of the machine. The man was just a function of the technology, a softer part of it.

Gradually he was connected up. His personal equipment connector, linking him to the oxygen supply, and the pressure system that inflated the g-suit in tight turns. Then the survival pack, with a dinghy and life-vest. His legs were restrained, in case of having to eject. The previous night Dave had drilled him again in ejection procedure; vital in an aircraft of this sort, flying low and fast.

'What was your all-up weight, sir?' said the crewman at his side.

'Two hundred and fifteen pounds,' Wolfe replied automatically, the figure having been running around his head all morning.

The crewman reached across him and dialled it into the controls, infinitesimally adjusting the aircraft's trim to accommodate him.

Four pairs of harness strapped him against the seat, clunking into a big buckle over his belly, and to tighten them he did as he had been drilled, and fidgeted roughly with his shoulders and hips, making the spring-loaded straps pull back on him and clasp him against the seat.

The moment he had been secretly dreading came next, as the crewman lifted up his bone-dome and lowered it gently on to his head. Again there was that sense of it being too tight, that if rammed down too hard his ears would be folded painfully flat, but somehow he eased them into place. The oxygen and radio leads were connected in place, finalizing his assimilation into the machine.

In front of him, and below him, Dave had long before completed his own settling in.

'How are you doing, John?' said his voice, startlingly loud in his ear.

'Fine, Dave. Thanks.'

He saw the helmet in front of him bob momentarily.

'No need to shout. The mike picks you up perfectly. And don't call me Dave. For the next hour I'm Red Two.'

'Sorry.'

He had been drilled on all that the night before. He and Dave, Red Two, were taking off from the SMA and rendezvousing with another Harrier from a dispersal point. That other Harrier was Red One. As soon as they had rendezvoused Red One and Red Two were going to take up standard defensive formation, fly-by over the centre of Delmira City—the daily goodwill blast, as the pilots called it—then head for a simulated bombing run somewhere in the Delmira hills to the west. One of the other Harriers on dispersal might or might not, depending on its own orders, launch a dummy attack on the formation during the flight. If so, they would take standard defensive action and try to shoot the marauders down on film. By standing Harrier practice, the attacking plane could *not* viff during the engagement—and thus simulate realistically the flying of every other fast jet the RAF would be likely to encounter in a shooting war—while the defending Harriers could, and certainly would, viff the attacker out of the sky.

The sound of their breathing was loud in John Wolfe's ears, but it was a sensation that was to be short-lived.

Dave said: 'OK, John, I'm about to start up.'

Lights glowed on the instrument panel in front of him, one of them indicating a fuel-pump. This was the only critical task Wolfe would have to perform in the air, as normally the navigator controlled the flow of fuel to the engine. By prior explanation, Dave had told Wolfe how to perform the task to his orders. Accordingly, Wolfe threw the switch, another light came on, and Dave thanked him.

Moments later, the engine started up. This was, or felt as if it was, about six inches behind Wolfe's seat. The Rolls-Royce Pegasus 103 develops 21,500 lbs of thrust, and in spite of his bone-dome helmet, Wolfe felt as if he was being deafened.

Around the plane, the ground-crew—now wearing soundproof ear-muffs—were snatching off the warning tags, which they then handed up to Dave, who stowed them away. Meanwhile, the pitch of the engine was building up, and the choking smell of aviation spirit was penetrating, even with the oxygen mask in place. There was a flurry of activity outside: the two ladders were snatched away, and hand-signals passed from the ground-crew were acknowledged in the same way by the pilot.

'All right, I'm closing the canopy. Keep your hands clear.'

The transparent dome of the canopy slid down from behind them, and as soon as it went into its seals the sound from the engine dropped off noticeably. However, deep vibration coursed through the machine, leaving no doubt about the power that was being delivered.

Dave's voice came through again: 'How do you feel?'

'Fine.' He was staring grimly ahead, over and beyond Dave's white helmet to the bright semi-circle of the open air, the runway, the ski-jump beyond. From here there was no returning. For good or bad, he was going to have to go through with it.

'OK, we'll be moving in just a moment. Don't forget, if I shout *"Eject!"*, head back against the rest, and pull hard on the handle between your legs. I won't call it twice. And I'll be asking you for fuel up-dates as we go along. You've got that?'

'Yes.' He added, too late: 'Red Two.'

Wolfe heard a squirt of tinny sound in his headphones; someone from outside talking to

Dave.

Dave said: 'Roger, Tower. Moving to launch point, then heading 27° at one thousand feet.'

At this point the engine revved up from what now turned out to have been its idling speed. A great roar and a howl came to Wolfe's ears through the canopy and bone-dome, frightening and exhilarating him simultaneously. The Harrier rolled forward to where a crewman beckoned them forward; he stepped aside smartly, and they carried on forward. Ahead of them was the ski-jump.

The plane accelerated. It accelerated, but it was a mild movement forwards, not the press of speed Wolfe had been bracing himself against. The engine was howling behind him, but the plane moved with awful slowness towards the ski-jump. Years of jet-travel had accustomed Wolfe to the violent thrust-forward of conventional flight, not this leisurely rolling.

The meeting with the gradient of the ski-jump caused the nose to tip up, the ground to vanish ... then a swooping sense of weightlessness followed by a slight sideways tipping to and fro, and at last a thrust of acceleration against his back. Clumping and banging came from beneath him. Looking sideways and down, Wolfe saw what he had accepted in his mind, but which his senses denied: they were already at least a hundred feet in the air and moving fast.

Red Two's voice, Dave's voice, was now calling over a number of checks: hydraulics, electrics, fuel (Wolfe was sufficiently alert to be able to read off the data), oxygen, engine, jet pipe temperature...

Another voice came in, identified as Red One, and in a moment or two, miraculously as it seemed to Wolfe, a second Harrier appeared over to their left, moving in the same direction but slightly ahead of them.

The ground was slipping by beneath them, tantalizingly fast, green forest and smears of water, paler masses of cane plantation; over to their right, the silver glimmer of the ocean. When the plane banked, turning fast, the g-forces pressed him down into his seat: he had been told to expect this, but nothing could have prepared him for the suddenness of the motion, or the strength of it. Wolfe felt helpless, as the world skidded madly by beyond the transparent canopy. Somewhere they must have over-flown the city, without Wolfe seeing it, because soon they were out over the sea, climbing fast, the engine howling behind him. He wrenched his head round, inhibited by the cramped cockpit and the hard helmet, and for an instant managed to glimpse the city spread along its coast. Then the plane banked again, the g-suit pressed his gut and his legs and his chest, and for several seconds Wolfe had no bearing at all.

When the plane levelled again, the nose

dipped and Wolfe could see, dead ahead and rising fast to meet them, the forested land. Red Two's helmet bobbed from side to side as he eyeballed the sky, but then he stared straight ahead as he brought the Harrier out of its bunt, and at about a hundred and fifty feet set off across the inland plains of Delmira. There appeared to be no distinguishing landmarks: rivers skidded by beneath them, so fast that there would be no hope of identifying them from the map.

Amazingly, or so it seemed to Wolfe, Red One was still visible, slightly ahead of them and to the left.

Radio silence was abruptly broken. 'Buster! Buster!' In Wolfe's headphones, Red Two shouted : 'Engage LRMTS!' The plane went into a steep turn—the land seemed to stand vertical outside—and g-forces once again thrust Wolfe into his seat. It was almost impossible to move his hands, and he could feel the soft flesh of his face bulging downwards. But the LRMTS (Laser Ranger & Marked Target Seeker) was operable from his seat, and the night before Dave had drilled him on its use. It was a highly specialized piece of equipment, one that needed proper training to use, but he was at least supposed to switch it on during this exercise. Another Harrier shot by, amazingly in sight for a second or two before flashing away. Wolfe reached over to the control for the LRMTS, painfully and slowly, then managed to switch it on.

'Can you give me a reading?' Red Two's voice rasped.

'I'll try.'

But the plane flipped over the other way, the horizon lurching from one kind of apparent vertical to another, and Wolfe could make no sense of anything on the panel in front of him.

'Hold tight!'

The warning was laconic and uninformative, giving no hint of what was about to occur. To this point, Wolfe had endured the movements of the plane with a sense of suppressed panic, knowing that he could do nothing to influence his fate. That much at least had put him in a suitable state of mind, but his body, particularly his gut, was in a state of upheaval. He was sweating copiously, and he could feel the oxygen mask loose on his dampened face ... but most of all he was convinced he was about to throw up.

Then the Harrier stopped dead, or seemed to. The engine made a racket, the plane seemed to kick up beneath him, and he hung forward in his constraining straps. The force of what happened could only be compared to hitting a cliff-face head-on. Outside, the horizon went crazy, the sky tumbled around them ... and to Wolfe's incredulous eyes, another Harrier appeared in front of them, weaving desperately to escape.

'Got him at six!' Red Two shouted, and then their Harrier banked away, accelerating and diving, while the horizon did its now normal trick of standing on its side.

During the engagement they had lost contact with Red One, and while they exchanged briefly on the radio (radio silence was maintained as much as possible), they roared at high speed over the jungle, seeming to skim the tree-tops. Quite quickly they came into hill country, and the plane was forced to weave through the hills and valleys.

Around them the hills became mountains, densely forested.

Wolfe heard the radio say: 'Roger Red Two.' Before he could work out what it might have signified, he noticed that the other Harrier had reappeared in its former position, slightly ahead and to the left.

Now the two aircraft held low over the mountains, trying to maintain an even height above the contours. It seemed they went faster and faster, hugging the ground more closely.

After the experience of sharp combat, and what he presumed was viffing, Wolfe felt this fast low flying was close to a normal way of life. It relaxed him—on a strictly relative scale—and he began to enjoy the flight for the first time. He knew that if the pilot made just one mistake then the plane would certainly smash against one of the mountainsides. There would not be a moment's chance of using the ejector-seat.

But Wolfe was keyed up, his senses alive to the experience.

In the comparative calm of this kind of flying, Red Two was able to speak to him.

'A few more minutes, John then we'll have to recover.'

'Recover?'

'We're moving to dispersal. We'll spend the night there, then after a short flight tomorrow, we'll return to the SMA.'

'All right.'

'You say Roger, when we're flying.'

'Roger.'

'Good. Would you mind switching fuel-tanks?'

'Roger,' John Wolfe said, beginning to feel like a qualified airman at last.

A few seconds later, their wing-man signalled that he was flying to dispersal point, the accompanying Harrier waggled its wings in signal, then soared away towards the south.

Wolfe's two-man Harrier continued on a north-westerly track, heading for the hills that straddled the border between Delmira and El Libertador.

CHAPTER TEN

A long chain of events, some of them occurring before he had even been born, had brought Captain Joe Nicholas of the US Marine Corps to Prudencia.

His father, Adalberto Nicolás, had been born in El Libertador, and lived in abject poverty on a smallholding for most of his young life. Extremes of starvation and illness had driven him to Prudencia to seek a better way of life, and he had fallen lucky. He soon found work shifting crates of beer for a brewery, and although he was at first physically weak, he soon gained strength and confidence. Within a year he had started his own business, making and selling crates, not only to the brewery that had first hired him, but to other businesses around the town.

Adalberto met and fell in love with Eloisa, daughter of one of his customers, and in due course they planned to marry. Everything looked good for Adalberto, but even in those days El Libertador was not politically stable. There was then a pretence of democracy, with a senate of elected elders, but they were mere functionaries for the whim of the President, a former Army officer called Carlos Limonta. President Limonta ruled the country with an almost total disregard for human rights. His secret police were hated and feared; he had created at least two opposing para-military 'peace-keeping' forces; his methods of taxation were feudal and without even a semblance of fairness; he and his family owned virtually all of the major businesses, and had a monopoly on the sugar-cane crop; political opponents, such as there were, frequently were murdered in public or tortured in secrecy; newspapers were heavily censored.

In all, the Limonta regime was barbaric and dictatorial, but it earned the discreet support of foreign powers because of its extreme, some would say fanatical, hatred of communism.

Adalberto Nicolás had never seen himself as a political man, but the fact was that the economic climate created by Limonta happened so far to suit him. Once he had abandoned the countryside for Prudencia, he had prospered.

But of course the Limonta regime was unstable, and ripe for overthrow. The inevitable coup d'état took place, Limonta was killed, his family exiled. *Limontistas* eventually made their own coup, a puppet president was installed, only to be killed in yet another coup. For the years that followed, El Libertador was probably the most unstable and unsafe country in Latin America. It was during this period that Adalberto decided that the economic climate no longer suited him, and he and Eloisa, and their two young children José and Dalia, one night filled a truck with their belongings and drove northwards out of Prudencia.

For the next year or two, Adalberto and Eloisa drifted slowly northwards, taking work wherever they could find it. They spent some time in Guatemala, but it was not long before they were in Mexico. For different reasons, times were hard throughout Central America, and in general people like Adalberto and Eloisa looked to the United States as the ultimate solution.

Inevitably, they reached the border, and equally inevitably they managed to get across one night. By this time Eloisa had two more babies, and their need to find stability and security was great.

Adalberto had not lost the initiative that had first helped him prosper, and he was quick to realize that as a family of Hispanic immigrants, living illegally in the States, he would be doomed to a shadowy way of life for many years to come. Wanting better for himself than that, Adalberto forced himself and his family to Americanize themselves. Almost from the first day he made his wife and children speak in English, even when alone, and the children's names were anglicized, along with his own. He and his wife became Albert and Louise Nicholas, their children became Joseph, Dorothy, Elizabeth and Alexander.

As a further precaution, Albert moved his family away from the southern US Spanish-speaking States—New Mexico, Texas, Arizona—and found work in Bloomington, Indiana. This quiet, mid-Western town accepted the young family without question, Albert soon found work, and from this by diligence established his own business. It was in this environment that young Joe Nicholas grew up.

Once the itinerancy of his childhood was behind him, Joe settled down and became a young American. By the time he was in his teens, he was distinguishable from his friends only by his Latinate good looks, his love of and active participation in a whole range of sports, and a remarkable ability with the Spanish language.

His relationship with his father was always close, and from Albert he acquired an independence of mind, a love of individual freedom and a hatred of repression in any form. Albert made no secret to Joseph of the family's background, but it was accepted that their past in Central America was forever behind them.

When young Joseph came to school-leaving age, his father accordingly did not try to influence the boy in any direction. He was therefore both surprised and delighted when he announced one day that he had decided to enlist with the US Marine Corps.

The Marines are the self-styled elite of the US armed forces. Battle-hardened in every war fought by the USA, they have a sense of identity and purpose unmatched anywhere. From the basic training of boot camp to his first commission, young Joe Nicholas was in his element. He asked and was given no quarter, he was popular and respected, and showed a toughness unequalled by his class.

But his single greatest virtue was the independence of mind instilled in him by his father.

So long as the training he was given and the orders he received were in line with his own thoughts, then everything went smoothly. He only ran into trouble when his own ideas were different.

He was intelligent enough to know when to draw the line, and so his rise in the Corps was smooth. He was a respected officer.

His undoubted qualities, plus his individual mind, made him a natural choice for the Air Wing of the Marines. He was selected for air-crew training, learnt to fly in record time, and became an outstanding combat pilot. He was eventually posted to a Marine ground-attack squadron, equipped with AV–8A Harrier jump-jets.

AV–8As were then new to the Marine Corps, and their full potential had not been realized. Joe Nicholas took to the planes as if born to them, and was the first in his squadron to make a Harrier viff, and consequently he spent several months training other pilots in their unique combat abilities. When he was flying, he was at the peak of his aptitude: intelligent, independent and motivated.

For old Albert Nicholas, the sight of his son achieving this level of skill was a vindication of everything for which he felt he had lived. He was proud of his other children, but Joey had become the embodiment of an ideal.

However, all was not exactly as it seemed. Just as a criminal psychopath can live undetected in a city for years, and do so simply by not realizing he is a danger to himself, so there was a potential in Joe Nicholas he did not know was there. It was a seed that had been planted in him during those long nomadic years of childhood.

By every appearance, Captain Joseph Nicholas was the all-American success story. By all accounts he was. In every level of his mind, bar the deepest and most unattainable, he wanted to *be* everything he *seemed* to be.

No one was more comfortable with Captain Joe Nicholas who flew Marine Harriers than Captain Joe Nicholas himself.

But because the seed of rebellion was undeniably there, it was inevitable that one day it would burgeon forth. That day was arriving.

It came, unexpectedly, with a call for

volunteers from a Washington-based Federal Aid Committee. Later, Nicholas was unable to trace the actual power-base of the Committee. Information came down through the structure of the Marine Corps, and consequently had an authority that could not be argued, but there was a certain vagueness that was at first discouraging.

What he found appealing, though, was that if he accepted the duty it would give him a chance to return to El Libertador.

All his adult life he had been haunted by the fragmentary memories of his childhood. He could recall the heat, the flies, the lazy way of life, the endless travelling, the forest-clad mountains, the sandy plains around the city ... but he could not remember anything in a coherent way; these images came sporadically and unconnected.

Also, his memory was romantic. His father looked back with nostalgia on his days in Prudencia, before the first of the coups, and Joe wanted to know the truth of the place.

Memories are like ghosts because they haunt you, but like ghosts they can be exorcised or laid.

Nicholas sensed that a return visit to El Libertador would help put this restless ghost to rest.

Accordingly, he did not enquire too closely about what his duties would be. He was told that he would be required to give advice to the Air Force in El Libertador, and perhaps oversee the re-equipment of their forces with new and superior machines. Joe guessed that an arms-sale was imminent, that perhaps the AV–8As were going to be sold to this country and that his expertise would be called for. He would receive his normal service pay while in El Libertador, plus what were described as generous living and accommodation expenses.

The trip would be regarded as having a security rating of Most Secret, and he would have to wear civilian clothes throughout his stay. These would be paid for by the government—though which particular government would pay was not spelt out.

Later, when Joe had accepted the commission, it was revealed fairly casually that his appointment had been made mainly because he was so proficient in Spanish. This was the first aspect of the arrangement that worried him, because not many of the men in his squadron could speak the language at all well. It seemed he had been lucky.

Only some weeks later did he start to think that he might have been picked out in advance, but by then he was in Prudencia and had met the local representative of—he presumed—McDonnell-Douglas. M-D were the American licensees of the Harrier, and in the weeks leading up to his departure Joe Nicholas had met not only the other Marine pilots who were on the assignment with him, but also a representative of McDonnell-Douglas who had given an entertaining lecture on the future development of the 'Big Wing' Harrier.

In Prudencia, chief of operations was an American called Charles D. Platten. Mr Platten seemed to have been briefed with the same background, which is how Joe Nicholas made his assumption about his employment.

However, nothing in the Prudencia operation had any formal or recognizable connection with the aviation company. Mr Platten was something of a mystery, and his precise function was . . . imprecise.

It was not long before Captain Nicholas became suspicious of what was going on. He had expected to be assigned to a unit of the Air Force, but instead he was checked in to a huge, modern hotel—which appeared to be almost completely empty of guests—and every day was asked to call in at the American Embassy for an up-date on his role in El Libertador. What this 'up-date' amounted to was a daily handout of expenses money: far in excess of anything he might reasonably be spending.

One day he approached Mr Platten directly, asking for something positive to do.

Mr Platten said: 'You're here as an adviser, Captain Nicholas. When we want your advice, we'll ask for it.'

Captain Nicholas's suspicions grew.

At the same time, with the long hot days spreading emptily around him, he needed to find something to do to fill the time.

Sometimes, he rented a boat from the harbour and went sailing with one or two of the other pilots. Sometimes he took a bus-ride into the countryside surrounding the capital. Both of these actions tended to be futile, as he was not a good sailor and the country around the city was bare and derelict.

So, day after day, Joe Nicholas walked the streets of Prudencia, on his own and away from supervision. In doing so he started to rediscover his childhood. He found streets, whole areas, which suddenly he recognized and remembered. He found the speaking of Spanish came naturally to him, as well as an almost instinctive grasp of the local dialect and slang. It was as if his Libertadorense background, suppressed all these years, was finding an outlet at last. He could feel his Americanness slipping away, even though, every evening, he returned to the company of his compatriots at the hotel and talked Marines and flying as if nothing had changed.

But something deep inside him *was* changing. He found that he was thinking in Spanish during the days, that he felt himself a Libertadorense, a Hispanic. His Latin temperament, suppressed over the years by schooling and training and the company he kept, started to emerge. His short-cropped hair began to grow, and he slicked it back in the way he saw the men in the streets slicked theirs back.

Every day, he ventured further into the backstreets of Prudencia, at first horrified by the poverty, filth and squalor, but later feeling an uncanny sense of familiarity. Once or twice he was hailed by passers-by, who evidently felt they recognized him, and this pleased him more than he could say, and in a way he could hardly fathom.

Several times he walked in the hills to the south of the city, those hills where the city spread out below, and where the poverty of Prudencia was worst. Here he fell into an introspective mood, almost as if by walking in a place where there was an overview of the city he could see it in deeper perspective in other ways.

Because he was a professional flyer he already knew the strength of El Libertador's Air Force. It consisted of a mere thirty combat aircraft, of which four were helicopters.

The remaining aircraft were Cessna A–37B jets. These were twin-engined aircraft, manufactured in the United States, based on a successful jet trainer, the T–37. As A–37Bs, the Cessnas had been sold to a number of small Latin-American countries, for use in counter-insurgency operations. The planes were light, fast and adaptable, capable of carrying a heavy

108

bomb-load as well as ground-strafing machine guns and cannon.

El Libertador was the sort of country that had no external enemies except the ones it made for itself. Its only threat was from within.

Any country, Joe Nicholas reasoned, that would equip its air force to defend itself from its own people, is a country divided against itself.

By his presence in El Libertador, as a servant of the junta, he was adding to the division. Whatever it was that he had been brought to this country to do, he liked the thought of it less and less.

Two weeks after his arrival in Prudencia, Captain Nicholas was told that he and the other pilots were about to be posted to the Santa Rosa air-base, where they would be conversion-training Libertadorense pilots to fast-jet combat. The El Libertador Air Force was in the process of acquiring a squadron of F–5E Tigers. That same day, Captain Nicholas was walking in the hilly squalor over the town when he came across a tiny row of slum dwellings and shops that he dimly remembered. While he was standing there, trying to remember, an elderly woman called from a shattered doorway:

'José! Hey! José Nicolás! You remember me! Come see me!'

And he went forward into his past, and later that evening he met a man from Cuba, and from that moment his life was changed.

CHAPTER ELEVEN

The flight was over almost as soon as it had begun. John Wolfe could not believe that they had been in the air for nearly an hour. He was just beginning to enjoy himself: his stomach was no longer on the point of eruption, he had three times manipulated the fuel-pumps correctly, he had managed at last to get the LRMTS working, and whenever the plane turned on its side he experienced a thrill of excitement, not of fear.

After separating from the other Harrier, Red One, Dave had taken them on a simulated bombing-run in the hills. The target was an abandoned paper-mill in a valley high in the mountains, and as they made their three fast approaches John Wolfe had operated the camera bomb-sight for a record of their hits. Dave was non-committal as to whether he thought they had been accurate or not.

Now they had continued on into the high passes, still turning and skidding through the tree-lined mountains, still hopping over crests and bunting down into the valleys, pulling up in time to slide over the next jagged summit, turning to the side, snaking along the courses of the silver river-beds. It was, for a fast fighter jet, a reasonably normal manner of travelling around.

In this state of relative relaxation, Red Two had been communicating by radio with the dispersal point they were circuitously approaching. The language was guarded, circumspect, and they spoke only in brief snatches. The exact locations of the dispersal points were carefully protected secrets, and Wolfe knew that the RAF changed them regularly.

Each dispersal base was a miniature RAF station hidden in the jungle. Its principal item was a portable, camouflaged hide for the Harrier. This was normally inflatable, for easy removal. Next most important was a portable ski-jump, which could be dismantled and re-erected at short notice. The aircraft needed a certain amount of improvised runway, and although sometimes strips of paved highway were used—particularly during NATO exercises in Western Germany—for real work in the field the RAF generally used PSP (pierced steel planking). This would be laid across the landscape, and although it was for Harriers much shorter than a normal runway—generally about 1,250 feet—it had all the disadvantages of a regular airport: vulnerability, and so forth.

However, the Harrier of course had real VTOL capability, so the short runway was only in use as a way of saving fuel and extending range. In a real shooting war, when the locations of the dispersed Harriers could literally mean the difference between victory and defeat, the aircraft would launch on the ski-jump, and return with VTOL. Noise apart, properly operated the dispersed base meant virtually incognito operations.

But this was peacetime, and the dispersal base to which John Wolfe's Harrier was returning was using the metal-strip runway.

In addition to the main requirements, a dispersal base had a number of ancillary installations. It had a ground-crew, and these and the air-crew needed to be catered for. So each site had to have tents, food, latrines, cooking facilities. And there were chairs and beds and tables. There were fuel-dumps, and ammunition dumps. An electric generator was needed, and in case of accidents there was emergency gear. The whole site—including the Harrier—could be moved by road, and for this there were three huge transporters. These too had to be dispersed and hidden in the forest.

It was a large operation to achieve a small thing: flying independence. But it was a small thing only in size: independence meant mobility, and mobility meant safety.

There were still a lot of organizational problems to overcome, especially concerning the still-new portable ski-jumps, but the RAF was emphatically not playing with dispersal sites. Delmira was an excellent place to rehearse or exercise the procedures, but in the front line of Europe, dispersal was a serious, crucial business.

People were beginning to understand what a Harrier squadron and its trained pilots could do. They were understanding, but Britain and her allies were years—literally, years—ahead.

While the US and the Soviet Union, and certain European powers, had repeatedly put the developmental emphasis on greater speeds, greater range, greater payloads, increasingly sophisticated computerization, more powerful missiles, and so on, the British Harrier had quietly turned its back on that sort of flying concept. It didn't go all that fast, it couldn't carry that large a weapons load, and nothing about it, apart from its engine, was all *that* revolutionary. Instead, it could outfly in air-to-air combat any other aircraft in the world, and it could land and take off from a shed in a wood. Its sea-borne cousin, the Sea Harrier, might have been what aircraft carriers were invented to carry.

After the war in the Falklands, half the militarized nations of the world were in the market for the battle-proved Exocet missile. The other half were anxious to get their hands on a few Harriers.

The Exocet missile was approaching obsolescence. The Harrier's military career had hardly begun.

Skimming along over the tree-tops of western

Delmira, Wolfe hardly had time to consider any of this, but it was all a part of his background briefing. He knew where he was going, and he knew why he was going there.

In the seat directly in front of him, Dave was speaking to the dispersal control, informing them of his position and direction of approach. The code-word came through that he was cleared for recovery, and then Dave's voice came through loud and clear in the headphones of Wolfe's helmet.

'All right, John. We're going in to land.'

'Anything I should be doing?'

Red Two said nothing for a moment, and Wolfe could see the white bone-dome nodding from side to side; that motion peculiar to the pilots of fast jets.

Then he said: 'No, just keep an eye open. And don't touch anything.'

This last was a reference to the weapons system; in the two-seat Harrier, many of the arming and guidance controls were in Wolfe's rear cockpit.

'I'll talk us down,' Red Two said suddenly. 'We're going for a RVL ... a rolling vertical landing. That means we'll hit the ground at about 40 knots.' He paused, and Wolfe saw the bone-dome waggle again. From where he was sitting he could just see Dave's hands on the controls. 'When we roll we don't run the risk of the engine picking up any muck from the ground. Could be inconvenient getting the engine fixed.'

RAF understatement, Wolfe thought.

'What would we really do if the engine was damaged?'

'The ground-crew would fit a new one. It's all part of the job.'

The plane banked sharply again, and Wolfe knew the short conversation had to end. Although he was 'eyeballing' the sky, as Red Two had requested, he had also been staring at the ground ahead, looking for the first sign of the dispersal base. He had no idea of how the pilot would locate it; the jungle ahead was its usual uneven sea of variegated greens.

The plane started to move with a different attitude: it was more nose-up (Wolfe found himself leaning forward instinctively, trying to compensate), and the engine was making more noise. There were clunks and thuds from below, and Wolfe guessed that the undercarriage had been lowered.

'OK, we're on full flap now ... taking her down...'

Suddenly, Wolfe's eyes made sense of the ground ahead. A narrow rift had been cut through the trees: geometrically straight in this forest of ungeometrically wild growth. Thus it was an obvious intrusion of technology into the wilderness ... but it was no wider than it needed to be, and it was no longer than it had to be, and so it was secure. A fast jet overflying it from the side would flash over it without its pilot having a chance even to glimpse it. Any other plane more than about 5,000 feet in the air would not be able to pick it out.

Only an aircraft coming in relatively slowly and relatively low, and approaching on the same line, would be able to find it.

The Harrier was now noticeably slowing, and behind John Wolfe's back the engine vibration was mounting. The plane had taken on an uneven motion, yawing slightly, together with an uneasy pitching.

But ahead of them, the metal track through the trees was clearly visible, and the jet was settling down towards it with a steady and deliberate motion.

Again, Wolfe had a feeling of unease about the plane's movements, based purely on his years of experience as a passenger in F–1011 Tristars and Boeing 747s. Taking off and landing were for him matters of forward speed: of great thrust on take-off, of a mad hurtling speed followed by noisy braking during a landing. Of course, he *knew* that he was in a VTOL, but this was not a matter of knowing, but one of feeling.

To him, it felt wrong to be passing over tree-tops at a speed less than he would drive his Mini down the M4.

Then they were no longer passing over trees,

but between trees, and the light of the sun was cut off.

At once, or so it seemed, there was the jolt of the wheels hitting the ground, and in the same instant Dave cut back the engine. Its noise fell away in a dying roar, as the plane rolled gently along the PSP. Ahead of them, two members of the ground-crew, each apparently clad in not much more than a pair of sandals, a pair of shorts and a pair of earmuffs, leaped out of the concealing foliage and signalled the pilot to keep rolling forward.

Dimly, at the end of the PSP, Wolfe could see the plane's hide. It consisted of wooden supports—presumably cut from local trees—plus a mass of overhead camouflage netting, with leaves and branches.

As the plane rolled onwards, taxiing in, he could see that beyond the hide were a number of tents, also discreetly camouflaged to blend in with the forest, as well as much equipment and stores, scattered around and painted dark green.

The canopy slid back, letting in the noise from outside . . . but also the fresh air. Wolfe slipped off his oxygen mask gratefully, feeling the air on his face. It was warm and humid, but after the cramped feeling inside the cockpit, and the sweltering humidity of the plains around the city, the tree-shaded dispersal base felt cool and refreshing.

Dave brought the plane to a halt outside the

hide, and a man on an electric bogey drove forward to hook up the undercarriage and swing the Harrier round, ready to be scrambled for its next flight.

'How do you feel, John?'

'Fine! When do I get another flight?'

'Steady on. We've got to be de-briefed before we can think of that. But I'll take you back to the SMA in the morning.'

As he was speaking the engine died away at last, whining down into silence. The bogey that had been hooked on gave a tug, the plane jerked and started a bumpy turning on its own axis, ready to be backed into the hide when the two men had climbed out.

Dave lifted off his own bone-dome, and handed it down to one of the ground-crew.

'You sit tight, John,' he said. 'There isn't such a large crew here at dispersal. I'll get you out of the cockpit myself.'

He released his straps, then with a wiggling motion of his hips raised himself up with his hands and stood on the seat. When the plane's turn had been completed, and a ladder brought up to the side, Dave climbed out backwards and went slowly down the ladder. He shifted it along to John's place, then climbed up again.

Meanwhile, the ground crewman walked away to help unhitch the bogey.

Dave stood on the ladder, looming up over Wolfe and reaching down to assist him. He

118

banged the buckle of the straps, and they wormed away into their sockets.

'All right,' he said. 'Try not to pull the ejector handle, but see if you can get your feet up at the same time as you shift yourself up.'

They were the last words he ever spoke. John Wolfe was complying with what Dave had said when the tranquil scene at the dispersal site was disrupted beyond recall.

A burst of loud explosions came from the trees over to Wolfe's left, and instantly Dave Hartford jerked with a violent motion, his head banging down on the rim of the cockpit. Then he jerked again, this time out and backwards, and Wolfe saw that half the man's head had been shot away. Dave fell backwards silently, and his body fell in a crumpled heap at the foot of the little ladder.

Meanwhile, a dazzle of noise and movement was going on around the Harrier. A group of men—Wolfe had no idea at first how many—had advanced into the clearing, and were sweeping it with bullets from fast-action automatic rifles held at their hips. The ground-crew, defenceless, were shouting and running, trying to escape ... but they were surrounded and unarmed.

Wolfe saw the man with the ear-muffs fall contorted on the PSP, a stitch-line of hideous bullet-wounds diagonal across his chest and neck. He twitched on the ground, then lay still.

Dark-brown liquid spread on the metal and undergrowth around him. Somehow, the fact that the ground-crew had been wearing only shorts made them seem that much more vulnerable.

Wolfe watched all this for the two, maybe three seconds in which it all began, not thinking of his own danger. But then something hit him hard on the top of the helmet, tugging his head to one side, and he realized how close he was to the flying bullets. He tried to sink lower in the cramped cockpit, but it was almost impossible.

Outside, it was a scene from nightmare. The ground-crew were being massacred. One of the attackers dashed away into the trees, shouting something in Spanish. Another followed. A crewman appeared from the other side, clutching a pistol. He was desperately working the mechanism as he ran, but the thing appeared to be stuck. Anyway, he never had a chance. Two of the attackers shot him, more bullets carving into him as he fell.

The noise was deafening, a barking crashing sound, a hateful explosive death. Wolfe had heard gunfire before, but always at a distance. There was a lull, and the two men who had run into the jungle returned, dragging an airman between them. He was still alive and unharmed. He looked up, saw Wolfe still sitting helplessly in the cockpit, and for a moment their eyes met. *My God, he's just a boy!* Wolfe thought in

horror, seeing a shock of fair hair, blue eyes . . .
and behind them, somewhere far away, a home
life with parents and a girlfriend, and a photo on
a mantelpiece of him in uniform with a shinily
peaked cap. And then the attackers thrust him
away, and shot him several times in the head as
he lay on the ground.

Suddenly there was silence.

No one moved, and Wolfe thought he was
going to be sick. He was transfixed by the sight
of the dead boy, the closeness of Dave
Hartford's body, the smoke from the rifles
drifting across the clearing.

Then the men turned towards him, holding
their weapons aimed in his direction, and,
thinking that death must soon be on him, Wolfe
raised his hands in a futile hope of being saved.

CHAPTER TWELVE

Luis Guedes was dozing in the cab when the
Cubano returned. He snapped awake at once,
remembering the harshness of the Cubano mood
when what they wanted did not happen at once.

The inside of the transporter's cab had
become a smelly place in the last day and a half,
partly because it was a small area for two people
to live inside for thirty-six hours, and partly
because of what those two people had from time

to time been doing. During the second day, as the temperature rose, both he and Rosaria had stripped off most of their clothes, and sat stinking and sweating together. Rosaria, in spite of Luis' best efforts to the contrary, was still *virgen*, but now he thought of the knowledge of him that her mouth possessed, and how once, briefly, she had allowed him the taste of her. But *virgen* she still was, holding the excitement for him of what might yet come.

By the time the Cubano returned, Rosaria had dressed again. She had taken a wash from their dwindling water supply, then slipped on her skirt and blouse and was lying in a bored way on the platform of the transporter. Luis dozed alone. Then their idyll was broken.

'Guedes!' It was the youngest of the Cubanos, Juan, a volatile and dangerous youth, destined no doubt for an early but spectacular death. 'Guedes! Get moving!'

He rapped peremptorily on the side of the truck with the barrel of his rifle.

'Where to? Where do I drive?'

'I'll show.' Luis heard Rosaria shout, and guessed that Juan had prodded or hit her with his rifle, to get her back in the cab.

'Get the engine going!'

Rosaria clambered up into the cab on the other side as Luis primed the huge diesel engine, then pulled at the starter. There was a long and mounting whine, and then the engine fired, belching out a huge black cloud of smoke from the stack overhead.

'Are you all right?' Luis shouted at Rosaria as she slammed the door.

'Shut up!' He glanced at her, and her face was set in the sulky expression she used when she most wanted to irritate him. He wondered what he could conceivably have done to deserve that.

Juan had clambered up on to the narrow foot-hold outside the driver's door, and was clinging on outside.

'Where's Mendoza?'

'He's waiting.' Juan signalled with his arm, needlessly, because he then bawled: 'Reverse up. Go back to the track we left!'

'All right.'

Luis shoved the truck into reverse, then tried to get his head out through the window to see what he was doing, but Juan was in the way, and showing no sign of shifting.

'I can't see where I'm going!'

'I will guide you.'

But the youth said nothing, and in a moment there was a scuffing, scraping noise from behind as the transporter reversed into the low-hanging branches of a tree.

Luis pointedly pushed open the driver's door, causing the Cubano to swing round to the front and out of the way. 'I can't see, kid!'

Expecting to hear the youth scream some obscenity at him, at the very least, or, more likely, simply kill him, Luis went forward a short way, then reversed properly the way he had come two nights before. In a couple of minutes he had got the huge articulated transporter back to the track.

Juan clung on, vagabond-style, as the truck moved off, but Luis, not liking the rough way he had been woken up, several times caused the truck to pass very close to branches and bushes, almost dislodging the Cubano youth. After he had done this a few times, Juan shouted at him to halt, then went round and climbed up into the cab.

Rosaria moved over to sit next to Luis.

The track Juan was taking them along climbed upwards through the trees, winding deviously through terrain that nothing but the largest vehicles could have crossed. Many times they went through shallow but fast-running fords, which the transporter took completely in its stride, but at other times the track was steep and the huge wheels lost traction.

At times like this, the truck came into its own: Luis selected the low-ratio, multi-wheel drive, and eased the great thing away from the slide. They climbed in this fashion for about half an hour, making slow progress all the way, and the track levelled out for a while, then began to descend. The noise inside the cab was no less for the advantage of the grade, for Luis had to stay in low gear the whole time, but now he could pick his way with less concern about getting stuck.

Juan was alert, pointing the way whenever the track diverged, then at last shouted excitedly and directed Luis through a screen of trees to where a wide path had been cut through the jungle.

'Now you reverse, OK?' said Juan, indicating awkwardly with his hands that Luis should turn the truck round before getting on to the path. Luis, still irritated by the volatile young Cubano, agreed and started the difficult and arm-wrenching job of turning the great machine in such a confined space.

Juan shouted something, then clambered out of the cab, and Luis thought the young man was going down to direct the turn. Instead, he ran off down the pathway in the direction in which Luis was supposed to reverse.

'You help me reverse up, eh?' Luis said to Rosaria, and the girl agreed. She too climbed down, but her instructions were unhelpful and almost inaudible. Muttering to himself, Luis managed to get the transporter turned round, and Rosaria climbed back up beside him.

Her hand slipped quickly to the inside of his thigh, and she gently squeezed his leg. 'Tonight we love again?'

'Sure,' Luis said, glad that that at least was something to look forward to.

He eased the transporter into reverse, and

125

took it down the path. Beneath the wheels, some kind of metal tracking had been laid in the grass.

He had his left elbow out through the driver's window, and his head above it, checking the transporter's clearance. Looking back to where he was reversing, he saw that the jungle cleared ... and that there stood the group of Cubanos, one of them beckoning with his hand as if to speed him up. Behind them was the unmistakable shape of a jet fighter-plane.

Luis stopped the truck a short distance from them, then got down.

He saw the bodies lying on the grass. He saw the plane's pilot, still dressed in his dull-green flying suit, sitting miserably on the ground.

'Holy mother of Jesus!' he said. 'What have you done?'

Rosaria was beside him, and she gripped his arm. She made a gasping noise.

Mendoza came forward.

'Keep your fucking mouth shut, Guedes,' he said. 'Get the plane loaded, and let's get out of here.'

'Are you *mad?* What do you want to steal a gringo plane for?'

Mendoza stepped forward, and swiftly and without warning slashed Luis across the face with the flat of his hand. 'I told you what to do. The gringos will be looking for us. We've got to get out of here.'

'Then let's go.' Luis backed towards the truck, holding Rosaria's hand. He had started to tremble, partly because of the impact of Mendoza's blow, but mostly because of the awful scene in which they had arrived: the motionless bodies on the ground, the smell of blood, the rifles held sheepishly still. Above all, the huge looming bulk of the jet plane, incongruously waiting behind them. The bombs that were slung beneath the wings seemed about to fall on them; the cannon mounted beneath the bulbous body seemed pointed straight at him.

Mendoza cocked his rifle, and pointed it calmly at Luis.

'The plane, Guedes. Load the plane.'

'OK, OK.' Luis ran back towards the truck, and behind him there was a shot. When he looked back he saw Juan standing with a rifle in his hands, the barrel pointed into the air.

CHAPTER THIRTEEN

Charles D. Platten, of New York City, was a moderate drinker, limiting himself to one martini before dinner each evening, and just a glass or two of wine during the meal. Sometimes, if he was away from the office or staying in an hotel, he might have a small nightcap, but in general he was frequently heard to claim that he was functionally a non-drinker and a non-smoker. In the latter case he was demonstrably accurate, and in the former relatively so.

He was not away from the office very often, believing that as his staff were expected to sleep on the premises then he should do so too. His room in his office was small but not spartan, so he had very little excuse not to. He did own a house in Prudencia, but for reasons of personal security it was several miles from the centre of the city, and because Prudencia was placed under a nightly curfew from 2200 hours—10.00 P.M., to Mr Platten, who said he disliked military nomenclature—it made movement difficult if he was needed suddenly at the office.

About once a month he was invited to the US Embassy for cocktails and a light supper. These were regular functions at the Embassy, to which most of the important US nationals in Prudencia were invited, in order to meet with one another informally, and to receive from the Embassy a certain amount of informal briefing on the US government's profile on one subject or another. Mr Platten, as a prominent member of the American community in Prudencia, always accepted these invitations (indeed, it is fair to say that these gatherings had originally been his idea), and not only received a little extra and confidential briefing, but had his own

128

information to pass to Embassy staff.

He did not tell them everything, however.

When attending one of these functions, Mr Platten invariably took a member of his staff with him for the sake of appearances. As with his sailing, he always took a woman member of the staff with him. She would wear the formal dress she had brought with her to Prudencia for this purpose, and Mr Platten would wear his dark suit.

Tonight, Mr Platten had with him a cipher-clerk named Rosemary Odell, originally from Springfield, Illinois, but lately from Washington DC. Rosemary, an intelligent and quietly spoken young woman, had been to one of these Embassy cocktail parties once before, and had agreed to attend a second time because of the food. She, like everyone else, grew tired of the convenience foods they had to eat at the office, and of the local food. At the Embassy you could be sure of good home cooking without any sense of guilt. She had only agreed in theory to attend; in practice, it was part of her duties and she had no choice.

While the aperitif cocktails were still being served, Mr Platten was taken to the office of the Air Force attaché, where he was given his latest briefing.

The attaché said: 'They've got one of the Brit Harriers.'

'Who is they?'

'The Cuban insurgents.'

'What do you mean, they've got one?'

'They went over the border, and snatched one.'

'Do the Brits know?'

'Do they ever! They're not pleased, Charles. Got any ideas?'

But Mr Platten was thinking of something else which was bothering him. Somehow he had neglected to mention this to anyone, but he was getting increasingly worried about Captain Joseph Nicholas, of the Marines.

'What do they want us to do?'

'Well, I've had a visit from the British Embassy, and they kind of feel we should be able to get it back for them.'

'Where is it?'

'Search me.'

'What about the government here?'

'Let's say that's why I'm talking to you about this, Charles. Maybe you could put a little pressure on them.'

It ruined Mr Platten's martini, having to think about the Brits. They made life difficult for him here in Prudencia, because committed as he was to stable and democratic government throughout the region, and equally dedicated to freedom under justice and an end to communist infiltration, but above all to self-determination without interference from outside, Mr Platten was forced into mental antagonism with the

130

British. From his point of view, their presence in Delmira was a destabilizing influence in the region.

Because the junta in El Libertador was, to put it nicely, against the British presence, and indeed had total claim on the Delmira territory, Mr Platten, as adviser to the regime, was committed to a similar viewpoint.

However, Mr Platten was a pragmatist, and much of his pragmatism concerning Delmira could be summed up in a few words.

Don't mess with the Brits.

It was Mr Platten's observed belief that the Third World was altogether too fond of taking advantage of the lenient views of the western democracies. Skilled Third World politicians could effectively get away with murder by exploiting the fact that western democracies did not, on the whole, declare war. Western democracies, being answerable at periodic intervals to their populations, felt constrained by popular opinion not to go and kick ass in small countries, even when those small countries were sticking their asses in the face of the world.

Thus it was, to take one small example, that the Ayatollah could take American citizens hostage inside their own embassy in Teheran, and not have to fear the consequences.

When, in 1982, the relatively small country of Argentina picked a fight with the relatively large

131

and powerful country of Great Britain—these terms being military ones—it had given Mr Platten an immeasurable amount of pleasure to see the Brits spit on their collective hands, roll up their collective sleeves, put on their collective hob-nailed boots, and proceed to kick the very shit out of the motherfucking Argentines.

Which were more or less his own words, modified only slightly.

Mr Platten had declared that the Brits had made the world a safer place. For a few years at least, he said, the West would not have to suffer the indignities of provocation.

However, it had not taken Mr Platten long to realize that the very same Brits were on his patch. His client government in El Libertador was, with his help ('advice' was his normal euphemism), arming themselves for a war with Delmira.

It gave Mr Platten a lot of mixed feelings.

The military attaché suggested that he and Mr Platten continued their talk after the light supper, and they returned to the dining room. Mr Platten sat with Rosemary Odell throughout the meal, but they did not have much to say to each other.

Afterwards, Mr Platten returned to the attaché's office, and at last felt able to bring up the delicate topic of the missing Captain Joe Nicholas.

What was peculiarly embarrassing to him was

that the Air Force attaché had not yet learnt that the Marine Corps had been proposing to sell its used AV–8As to El Libertador, and that Captain Nicholas and the other pilots had been sent to the country to teach—i.e. *advise*—the junta's men how to fly Harriers.

The Brits weren't going to like that. Mr Platten discovered that the Air Force weren't exactly delighted about it, either.

'Now let's get this straight,' the Air Force attaché said at the end of it all. 'The Brits have lost a Harrier. We've lost a Harrier pilot. That right?'

'That's right,' said Mr Platten.

'Then I guess we can say the two are connected, right?'

'Right,' said Mr Platten.

When Mr Platten left the office, he found Rosemary Odell in the main lobby, waiting for him. She was alone.

She said: 'Mr Platten, it's a quarter after ten. The curfew has begun.'

'We'll get us a car.'

'It's not possible.'

'Then we'll stay the night here.' Mr Platten stared thoughtfully at the floor for about thirty seconds. 'No, we'll get us a car.'

The US government, careful of its relationship with the El Libertador regime, did not allow its embassy cars on to the streets after the curfew; it did, however, own two or three unmarked cars, and this was a fact Mr Platten was well aware of. It took another twenty minutes or so of wrangling, but it was important he should get back to his office that night, and in the end he was given the use of one. With Rosemary Odell driving, and Mr Platten in the rear, the car eased its way as quietly as possible out of the embassy compound and headed for the backstreets area where Mr Platten had his office. It was not Mr Platten's night. Two blocks from their destination, an Army Jeep (ex. US, as Mr Platten knew only too well) drove them into the side of the road, its tall FM antenna waving to and fro. Mr Platten reached into his billfold and took out his pass.

Four soldiers climbed out of the Jeep, and sauntered menacingly towards the car.

Rosemary Odell said: 'What should I do, Mr Platten?'

'Just leave the talking to me. I got clearance.'

But as he wound down his window, he heard the scream of pop-music coming from the Jeep's radio and saw that two of the soldiers were smoking. One of them, unshaven and breathing heavy fumes of alcohol and garlic, leaned down by Mr Platten's window.

'*¡Andiamos!*' he said, jerking a filthy thumb. 'Get out of the car!'

'Here,' said Mr Platten, showing the pass.

The soldier swung his arm, knocking the pass out of Mr Platten's hand so that it fell, unread, on the ground. 'Get out of the car! And the woman.'

'Do what they say,' Mr Platten said.

'Yes sir.'

He and Rosemary Odell got out of the car, but the moment they did so the four soldiers moved quickly against them. They were separated: Mr Platten was turned around and pushed forward face-down across the roof of the car, and Rosemary Odell against the wall of a nearby building.

Mr Platten, realizing that none of the men was an officer, and thus without reading the pass would have no idea who he was, asked to be taken to a senior officer. The answer he got was the stock of a rifle smashed painfully down on his spine and kidneys, causing him to bellow with agony. One of the soldiers grabbed his billfold, and emptied it of its cash.

Then Mr Platten was allowed to turn, and held back against the car he was forced to watch what the soldiers did to Miss Odell.

She was being held by one of the soldiers, who had crooked one of her arms behind her back, and had his arm compressed tight against her throat. Her head was bent backwards. The other soldier, using a knife, had cut away her dress, letting the top half of it fall about her waist. As Mr Platten watched, the soldier slid his hand into each cup of her bra, then down the front and back of her pants. Miss Odell could barely breathe, let alone scream for help.

She could, however, move her legs, and she brought out knee sharply up into the man's groin. The response was immediate. The two men beat her to the ground, and kicked her in the head, chest and stomach.

Meanwhile, the announcer on the radio praised the singer of the last record, played an advertisement, then put on a new record.

When the soldiers had finished with Miss Odell, she was semi-conscious and bleeding. Her bra had been torn away, but in a show of belated prudery, one of the men dragged the remains of her dress over her to cover her bruised nakedness. She lay still, one arm covering her head.

The four soldiers then turned to Mr Platten, and proceeded to beat him up. He had been hurt but not injured when the sordid incident was brought to a timely end. A second Jeep miraculously appeared in the silent streets, its tyres screaming as it raced around the corner. This too carried four men, unsupervised by an officer, but their arrival was enough to bring Mr Platten's beating to an end. As he lay by the sidewalk, groaning with pain, the two Jeeps accelerated noisily away, the sound of pop-music vanishing into the night.

Miss Odell and Mr Platten got back to their office with no further incidents, but Rosemary was badly hurt with three broken ribs, broken teeth and internal bleeding. She returned to Washington two days later.

Mr Platten was busy in the days following this, but he was soon relieved to hear—though not vindictively, of course—that the four soldiers involved in the incident had later disappeared mysteriously from their barracks, and were never seen again.

At Mr Platten's suggestion, the curfew was changed to begin at 2300 hours—11.00 P.M.— but like the earlier one, there were usually ways around the inconvenience that was caused.

But it was a minor distraction; the disappearance of a British Harrier and an American Harrier pilot were soon Mr Platten's dominant problems.

CHAPTER FOURTEEN

Luis Guedes felt as if he had been cheated. Had he not, after all, made an epic journey through the forest for the Cubanos, for Los Enfadados? Had he not loaded the gringo plane aboard his transporter without damage to either? And had he not then driven the precarious load through dense trees, screamed at all the time by Mendoza who wanted more speed? Never had he carried such a load. Never had he carried a load balanced so narrowly on wheels.

And now the Cubanos had taken Rosaria away from him; his prize, his payment. Maybe now, his love.

After the shocks when he arrived in the clearing, there had come the surprises. One was to discover that the gringos had transporters rather like his, used to carry the plane and its equipment from one place to another. Luis had believed that the one he drove was the only one in Central America, yet the *ingleses gringos* had some too.

And when they left the bloodied site, with the Harrier chained in place, the Cubanos had directed him a different way, along the route the gringos used to carry their equipment to and fro. This was a way no less steep than the way he had come, but it was clear that it had been carved from the jungle in such a way that not only was it concealed from the air by the overhead spread of branches and leaves, but that around the track itself, the trees' lower branches had been cut back to allow a heavily loaded transporter to move without damage to its load.

So, for the first few kilometres, the way through the forest was clear. But such clearing had been made only on the Delmira side of the border. It was important that the gringos should not know where they were, but it was equally important not to stay in Delmira! Soon the Cubanos directed Luis away from this track, and the way became difficult and slow.

Many times they were forced to stop while a way was cleared for the aircraft. It was inevitable that it would get scratched and knocked about, but the Cubanos made it plain that the aircraft must not be seriously damaged.

Luis was forced to use every particle of skill and experience he possessed in driving the transporter across the border; no one complimented him on what he was doing, Rosaria was not there to squeeze the inside of his thigh, but even so Luis felt a sense of quiet satisfaction from a job well done, a professional task accomplished.

But to hear Mendoza scream at him whenever they were forced to stop, you would think Guedes had never before driven anything bigger than a Fiat! Luis felt a familiar sense that his body had expanded to include the bulk of the great truck and its load, that he had become the machine. As the transporter bumped and skidded along the track, and the branches and trunks scraped the painted metalwork of the aircraft on its back, Luis felt the grazes as if they were on his own skin.

But at the end, when his work was done, it was taken completely for granted.

Night fell suddenly, making any further driving extremely dangerous: not only for the truck and its precious load, but also for the people who were forced to ride on the back. Only Mendoza and one other Cubano were in the cab with Luis as he drove. The other three men, Rosaria, and the captured gringo pilot were on the platform, clinging on.

Mendoza, obviously annoyed by the forced halt, said they would camp overnight, and organized the men into guards. It soon became clear that the gringo pilot would be watched all the time, Luis some of the time.

Thus Luis sensed that his state of being a semi-prisoner continued.

Mendoza went to the water-tank, and Luis watched in the dim glow from the truck's lights. The water came out, but only in a trickle.

Mendoza rounded on Luis: 'Where is the water? This was full when we left!'

'We drank it . . . it was hot.'

Luis thought of Rosaria's young body, washing down negligently in the warm trickle from the tank. He said nothing.

'This has to last us! What happened? What did you do?'

'You said nothing about it. We used it.'

Mendoza was advancing on Luis accusingly, anger blazing in his eyes. But then Rosaria pushed forward.

'I used it for washing!' She stood before him defiantly. 'Who cares? The jungle is full of water!'

What followed shocked Luis to the core. Mendoza grabbed a rifle from one of his men, and clubbed Rosaria with it, catching her where her shoulder met her neck. He must have pulled the blow just before it hit because it merely knocked her to the ground. Stunned more by the action than by the effect of it, Rosaria climbed to her feet. She advanced on the Cubano leader, her hands clenched like claws.

'I'll kill you for that!'

Mendoza raised the rifle again, but two of his men grabbed hold of it and jerked it away from him. He glanced at them, then walked forward to meet Rosaria. She flew at him, hands scrabbling for his eyes and hair, but Mendoza was trained. He hit Rosaria hard and expertly: one fist across the side of the head, another in her side, a sharp brutal kick against her hip . . . and as she fell away, he caught a handful of her hair and held her head like that, while his hand went flat across her face, to and fro, four, five, six times, knuckles and palm in quick succession.

Then she fell on the ground, and he turned away from her. He was breathing heavily, his shoulders shaking.

The other men—Cubanos, Luis, the gringo pilot—stood in shocked silence by the speed and brutality of the attack.

Sensing this, Mendoza said: 'Tonight we all have a party, hey?'

But the eighteen-year-old girl who was, presumably, to be the centre of any such party, was unconscious on the overgrown soil of the forest.

Luis said: '¡*Bastardo*, Mendoza!' He went forward and crouched by Rosaria. She groaned, and he held her tenderly.

That long night passed uneasily, Mendoza cut off from the other men by his actions. The guard was maintained on the gringo pilot, who anyway seemed still in shock from the first attack, but the earlier sense of unity of action had dissipated.

It was restored at first light, as the men were waking up and preparing to continue the long trek through the forest. There was a distant, alien sound, growing quickly nearer, getting louder, but which then faded away as soon as it had come. Glances were exchanged. Then there was a second sound, closer and louder, unmistakably that of a jet aircraft, one travelling low and fast.

It shot overhead with a deafening row, and departed.

Suddenly, the Cubanos were grinning. Juan, the youngest, picked up his rifle and fired several rounds into the air.

'The gringos are looking for us!'

Only the captured pilot looked apprehensive and tired. Everyone piled aboard the transporter, and Luis selected the gear.

The end of the journey came around midday, when the air was sultry and humid and almost unbreathable. Mendoza was directing, when suddenly there was a banging on the roof of the cab, followed by indistinct shouts. Mendoza grinned at Luis, and pointed over to the left.

The track led down through trees, but now it was wider than before and freer from obstruction. The ground fell sharply away to the right, rose equally sharply to the left. Young trees grew on each side, still giving cover. Looking down, Luis could see that they were descending into a deep pit along a road built across the face of the wall. It was obviously some kind of old quarry, long since abandoned. The road twisted down, curving round precipitously, heading for the quarry floor.

This was bare for much of its extent, but on the far side a good number of young trees had sprung up, affording cover. Mendoza directed Luis across to these trees, and with now practised movements, Luis manoeuvred the transporter and its extraordinary load into the shade. The other Cubanos were already jumping off the truck, and two of them stripped off their clothes as they ran, leaping head-first into a huge pool that spread at the base of one of the cliffs.

When Luis turned off the engine, a great humid silence surrounded him. It was shaded under the trees, but it was hot and airless, a great stillness permeating the hiding-place. Birds shrilled overhead, scattered through the trees, and on the overloaded air there was the pervasive perfume of flowers.

Luis clambered down, and found Rosaria—bruised and silent from her ordeal, but otherwise now unharmed—waiting for him. She slipped an arm through his, and pressed herself against him. Ignored by all the others, they walked over to the pool and sat down together by the water.

CHAPTER FIFTEEN

A modern warship, given sufficient motive, will move through the seas at an extraordinary pace. It is slowed only by its accompanying flotilla, because in the modern age no warship can operate alone. Thus it was that HMS *Invincible*, finished with her NATO duties in the Sea of Japan, was heading south through the Pacific Ocean, on her way to a goodwill visit to Hawaii, when the signal arrived announcing the loss of the Harrier and the murder of her crew.

Invincible's Master sent a signal of goodwill and regret to the people of Hawaii, and steered a more south-easterly course, adding a few knots to her already formidable pace. Meanwhile, HMAS *Australia*, formerly the *Hermes*, set out northwards from her base in Brisbane; a show of support from the Commonwealth. HMS *Ark Royal*, a newly commissoned light aircraft-carrier of the *Invincible* Class, happened, quite by chance, to be paying a goodwill visit to Jamaica, and in no time at all she was moving south-westwards through the Caribbean, showing the flag for Delmira. It was not a task force and was not intended to be one, but no ship of the size of these capital vessels would or could sail without an accompanying support fleet. This would generally consist of at least one destroyer, two or three anti-submarine or anti-missile frigates, a squadron of Sea King or Lynx helicopters, and the Royal Fleet Auxiliaries to supply them all.

In spite of a deliberate running down of the Royal Navy by successive post-war governments, the British could still muster the third largest ocean-going fleet of warships in the world. Before the Falklands war, the Royal Navy had 62 major surface combat ships, plus a fleet of 28 submarines, nearly half of which were nuclear-powered; this was quite separate from the strategic missile-carrying Polaris submarines.

After the war, in spite of persistent and habitual government pussyfooting, the Royal Navy had increased in number and strengthened in firepower.

There were now three fully operational *Invincible* Class carriers: the *Invincible* herself, the *Illustrious* and the *Ark Royal*. Each of these, in normal times of peace, carried 5 Sea Harriers,

12 Sea King helicopters and Sea Dart or Sea Wolf missile systems. The destroyers and frigates sunk in the Falklands operation had been or were being replaced; other ships due to be sold or scrapped had been retained.

A lot of hard lessons had been learned from the Falklands: that British aluminium warships burnt with horrifying speed, that Exocet missiles, and their military equivalents, were a major threat, that low-flying jets lobbing old-fashioned bombs were as much of a danger as they had always been, but that a massive retaliation from shipboard machine-guns was as effective as they too had always been.

Above all, perhaps, that the British sea-borne Harriers were something that had no equivalent anywhere in the world.

Within a few days of the massacre in the Delmira jungle, the two British capital ships were cruising in international waters, below the horizon, one off the Delmiran coast to the east of the Central American isthmus, one off the El Libertador coast to the west. The Australian ship would be on-station a few days later. Other ships were on stand-by.

Signals went out to C-in-C Fleets, in Northwood, Middlesex, and soon the gist of them was on the desk of the Minister of Defence.

★   ★   ★

Governments, like ships, appear to travel slowly, but can cross considerable distances under the cover of night.

The sort of night democratic governments habitually use is the one of misdirection. What they do is to seem to do nothing in the form of the sort of action called for by, say, the press and television. Then to say, in the same newspapers and on the same television, that they *are* doing exactly what they should be doing. And finally, actually to do something else.

The story of the murder of the seven men, and the sensational theft of the fully operational two-seat Harrier, broke suddenly and spectacularly in Britain.

The actual discovery was made by the crew of an RAF Wessex helicopter, despatched from the SMA near Delmira City on a routine investigation flight after the crew at Dispersal Site DF-5 had failed to radio in at the routine time. Such investigation flights happened frequently, as communication between DF and SMA were one of the continuing operational problems.

The story was released in London some five hours later (a delay which eventually brought the government's handling of the crisis into question); by then, it was 8.00 A.M. in Britain, just in time to catch the morning news bulletins

147

and the then-new breakfast TV programmes.

The first version of the story—containing a certain amount of guesswork—was that the pilot and the plane had gone missing, and the ground-crew had been murdered in a separate incident. Then it was revealed that the pilot was among the dead, and it was assumed that the plane was either still on the ground, or that it had been destroyed.

By the evening of the same day, the whole story was known, the only remaining mystery being who had taken the aircraft, and how. Again, it was first assumed that the plane had been flown out by a trained pilot, but later forensic evidence from the site revealed that a heavy-duty transporter with hydraulic lifting gear had been used. The trail was followed as far as the border with El Libertador, where it was lost.

Later the same day, local time, the RAF began regular intrusions into El Libertador's air-space, on low-level search missions.

It was these, rather than the theft of the aircraft itself, which began the diplomatic row between Britain and El Libertador.

Britain demanded the return of the Harrier, plus the extradition to Delmira of the men responsible for the crime.

The junta in Prudencia complained to the UN about British aircraft overflying El Libertador sovereign territory, and, furthermore, renewed its claim to the 'occupied' land of Delmira.

The President of the USA called for immediate negotiations.

The UN Security Council met to discuss the situation.

All this went on in full public view, but in Britain there was a strong groundswell of popular opinion with rather less interest in the niceties of diplomacy. Headlines in the tabloid press quickly reflected this opinion, urging the government to march into El Libertador and grab back the Harrier.

Thus began the time-honoured procedure by which the government placed night about its activities, and steamed forward.

★ ★ ★

Mike Shelley said: 'Foreign Secretary, the public are calling for action. Why don't we send a task force to Delmira?'

'The problem is, a task force against whom? The government in El Libertador is taking the line that we have deliberately created this situation for political reasons. They claim the Harrier is not on their soil.'

'Nevertheless, I take it that it is?'

'There is nowhere else it could be. Of course, it's very tempting to think that we could march across the border in force to look for it, and I've a lot of sympathy with those people who want us

149

to do just that. It may come to it in the end, of course, but for the moment we have to pursue a diplomatic solution.'

'So you don't rule out the use of force?'

'Oh no. We have made it quite clear from the outset that we will not hold back when the time comes. This is why we are overflying El Libertador and making sorties into their airspace. They must know that we mean business.'

'Foreign Secretary, how much credence do you give to the idea that for once the junta might be telling the truth? That they really aren't responsible for this?'

'I take it you mean the theory that Los Enfadados are somehow behind all this?' Shelley nodded. 'Well, it's a possibility, but from what we know of Los Enfadados, they would not have the material resources to pull off a coup of this sort. You have to remember that we really know very little about this supposed group of insurgents. In fact, everything we do know comes directly or indirectly from the regime itself. It's quite common in countries ruled by the military, for the regime to exaggerate the strength or influence of armed guerrilla resistance as a way of taking some of the responsibility from themselves for things that go wrong. It's sometimes convenient to have a scapegoat.'

'Then you do not believe that the Cubans

have been supplying aid to the guerrillas?'

'No.'

'And there's no chance that a Harrier might be about to fall into Soviet hands?'

'No, and I'm glad you've raised that. There's been talk about this missing Harrier as if the plane were top secret. There's no secret about the Harrier itself, and like any modern warplane it's dependent on a complex network of spare parts and servicing, both highly specialized, and so although we don't particularly want to see one of these things fall into the wrong hands, even if it did so it wouldn't be much use to them.'

'But it *is* a special aircraft.'

'Oh yes ... and we're extremely anxious to get it back undamaged.'

'So, if I may re-cap, Foreign Secretary, you believe that it is the El Libertador junta who are responsible.'

'Yes, that must be the case. Whoever has committed this crime, if the plane is on El Libertador territory, and we have every reason to believe it *is*, then ultimately it becomes their responsibility.'

'And if they won't hand it back to us. . . ?'

'We're working on the assumption that they will.'

'But if they don't . . .'

'It's my job to see they will.'

'Foreign Secretary, I must press you on this.

What is the British government going to *do* if the Harrier is not handed back?'

'Well, of course we should have to use force. But let me assure you, we are a long way from that.'

'One last question, Foreign Secretary. I think we are all anxious about the fate of the missing journalist, John Wolfe. Do you have any reassurance for his family and friends?'

'We have no firm news. I must tell you that straight. But we believe that because his body was not found with the others then he must be alive and well. We think he is being held hostage. Your viewers can be certain that we are pursuing the El Libertador government on this as a priority.'

'Thank you very much.'

The studio floor-manager had been signalling to Mike Shelley to wind up the interview, and so he made his closing remarks, the lights went down, the credits were played.

Later, in the hospitality suite, Mike said to his old friend: 'Chas, you ducked it. Are you going to send in the troops?'

The Foreign Secretary grinned, and sipped his gin and tonic.

'I'll tell you what, Mike. If you don't ask me that again, I'll tell you something else you'd like to know.'

'What's that?'

'The date of the next election.'

Mike Shelley laughed with his surprise. 'Only the Prime Minister can—'

'That's right, and so it's just an educated guess. The date will be about three weeks and four days after we get that bloody Harrier back.'

The governmental ship was in full steam.

CHAPTER SIXTEEN

From the journal of John Wolfe:
May 18.

For some reason they did not search me, and so I still have my notebook and pen, both found where I had put them what seems like an eternity ago: in the knee-pocket of my g-suit. I did not bring much with me because Dave Hartford advised me not to. Now I wish I had brought all sorts of stuff with me!

I would like to clean my teeth; I would like some fruit; I would like a change of clothes; I wish I had some chocolate, or something to chew. I wish I wasn't here.

'Here' seems to be an old quarry, a perfect place to take us, and obviously chosen in advance. I could easily get up the track to the surface, as it's a shallow gradient, but (a) I'd probably be shot before I got a quarter of the way up, and (b) where in hell are we?

I've been trying to figure out our approximate

position. The truck was going for an afternoon and a morning, but did not travel at night. It never went above about five or ten miles an hour, and for at least half the time we were actually stationary while they cleared branches. Also, we did a lot of doubling back. We can't be more than about thirty miles from the RAF dispersal base, and less than that as the crow flies.

Presumably, we have crossed the border ... but which one? Dave carefully didn't tell me whereabouts the dispersal site was, and Delmira has land-frontiers with El Libertador, Guatemala and, I believe, a sort of point of contact with El Salvador in the south. So that's out, and as I know we were flying north at the end of the mission, my guess is El Libertador. But why?

And what in God's name do they want a Harrier for?

My Spanish was never good when I'm on the receiving end. I'm like a lot of the British, in believing that foreigners all speak too quickly. Fortunately, I can make myself understood in it, and I've managed to convey to them what was pressing on me. That is, I'm not a pilot. I think it was this that saved my life, frankly. They got Dave and spared me, thinking I was the pilot ... but if they'd got ideas about me flying the Harrier, they had another thought coming. I told them I was a trainee pilot, and they

154

accepted that without threatening to kill me. From what I could work out, they've got someone here who can fly a Harrier.

Dave Hartford. I'm still numb with shock from what happened. I hardly knew him, but he was friendly to me as if we'd known each other for years. I'll never forget the way he died: the suddenness of it, the blood, the awful noise his body made as he died. Then that whole shooting business: the noise and smoke, the kid being shot in cold blood. It had an unreal quality to it, but only because to accept it emotionally as real would give the system too great a shock. When I get out of this, when I get back, the first thing I'll do will be to write a proper article about Dave Hartford, how he died, everything. I owe that to him. And I'll find out the names of the others, do my best by them, for whatever that's worth.

Notes on who I'm with: There are five or six bandits; the number is uncertain because one of them—the driver of the truck that got us all here—is obviously at odds with them, is scared stiff of them, and seems to be as much of a prisoner here as I am. I haven't found out his name yet. The leader of the gang is a big guy called Mendoza. He looks like Hollywood's idea of a psychopath, which means, of course, that he is no such thing. I'd guess he's had army training somewhere: he's a tall, broad, well-muscled man, obviously as fit as hell, walks like a panther, doesn't smoke (the others all do), and has the sort of keen functional intelligence that makes someone like him brilliant at the job he does, but not for much more. He was one of the two who shot the boy.

The other four don't have much to say for themselves, and I haven't caught their names yet. One of them drinks a lot, without seeming to get drunk (there was a cache of food and stuff here when we arrived, which points to preparations), another looks very young, another keeps spitting out nasal mucus, and so on. I'm scared of them all for the usual reasons, particularly because I've seen what they're capable of with their guns. They don't joke much, and the only fun they seem to have is strutting up and down with their rifles, and scrapping with each other. They do that a lot, like young dogs showing off their strength. And they do it especially when the girl is around.

Her name is Rosaria. I'm not exactly sure how she got involved in all this, but her presence sets up some interesting pressures on us all. I actually feel about as randy as an old shoe—being kidnapped has that sort of effect on you, I've discovered—but the other men seem constantly aware of her. They are always glancing at her to see reaction to anything that goes on.

She got pretty badly beaten up by Mendoza on the first night, and her face, arms and one of her legs are badly bruised. But she's obviously in good health because the bruises have started to fade already, and the swelling has gone down. Looking at her objectively—which, in this old-shoe state, is all I'm good for—I'd say she's reasonably pretty, and has an attractive young body, but I can't say anything about her intellect or opinions because I haven't talked to her. She has a sort of sulky blow-hot, blow-cold sensuality, which these men obviously find a big turn-on, but which leaves me pretty much unmoved. She seems very young, is all I can think. She's wearing a thin white blouse with nothing on underneath, and one of those loose skirts they wear round here, also with nothing on underneath, at a guess. She's found a shawl from somewhere, and clutches it around her constantly, in spite of the heat.

The two men I most worry about are Mendoza and the young one. Mendoza because he knows what he's doing, the kid because he doesn't. A deadly combination, as I saw at the dispersal site, because the kid was the one who shot the boy in cold blood.

Fashion note: everyone here, except the girl and the driver, is wearing Levis and T-shirts. Mendoza has a combat-jacket, which he wore for a time—probably to impress me or the girl—but he hasn't worn it since we've been in the quarry.

Catering note: chilli beans and some kind of

anonymous minced meat. Hot as hell, burns its way down your gullet, lies like a fire-brick in your gut, then emerges later as burning-gas farts or red-hot shit. Needless to say, the indigestion I was getting in Mexico City has started up again.

I keep remembering how Dave used to warn me never to eat beans before flying, because they make you fart.

★   ★   ★

May 19.
There was a lot of business today with the Harrier. All I can think is that they're seriously intending to fly it, although how, where to, to do what, etc. etc., I really can't think. I keep breaking out in a cold sweat about this, because I'm not sure about my position on this.

Yesterday I told Mendoza that I couldn't fly the thing, and he seemed to accept that. But today he told me he wanted me to check it over and see if it had been damaged. My position is ambiguous on this. I was spared in the shoot-out, and Dave wasn't, and I don't know if (a) they meant to shoot me but simply missed, (b) they thought I was the pilot and needed me for something or (c) they know I'm not a pilot and want me for something else. I've decided to keep a low profile on this until I know a bit more.

When Mendoza told me to check the plane out, I said at first I didn't need to (*translation:* I didn't know how to), but then he turned a bit ugly and so I played along with the gag.

I walked all around the plane, banging a hand knowledgeably against the sides and the wings, peering up into the undercarriage recesses, and so on. Then I leant down into the cockpits and joggled the straps a bit, then pronounced the aircraft sound.

In fact, the plane was in perfect working condition when we landed, and provided it wasn't hit by a stray bullet during the shooting, it should still be the same. I had a good look, and couldn't see any holes. A few smears of blood, which I'd wiped off.

Earlier, the plane had been lifted down from the truck, and shoved into the shade of the trees. This was a long and noisy operation, although most of the noise came from people shouting. The driver, whose name I've discovered is Luis, seemed to know what he was doing, and in spite of everything, he got the plane lifted safely down.

Now it stands like an immense bird, proud and beautiful, and horribly out of place in this dump.

There was another row about the truck. It turns out that Luis was forced to steal the transporter, or somebody else stole it for him, and he wants to return it. They talked him out

159

of that. Then he changed his tack. He said, as far as I could follow the argument, that it was nearly out of fuel. They said it didn't matter, he said it did. Apparently, using the hydraulic lift gets through a lot of diesel. I gather they don't want him to take the plane anywhere else, but he might have to do some more lifting.

In the end, he left to go and fill up with fuel. That was about mid-afternoon. To make sure he comes back, they made him leave the girl here ... and when this was made clear to him he almost changed his mind about going. In the end, he pushed her towards me, and told me to look after her.

Although what I can do in my position is beyond me. Anyway, she's with me now, following me everywhere I go. I think she's genuinely scared stiff of these bandits, and with good reason, but doesn't hold a grudge against Mendoza for beating her up. She doesn't have much to say to me, but apparently prefers me to the others. Or, to put it more accurately, distrusts me less than the others.

Tonight, she and I found a place to lie down for the night: I've cut some long grass from the pool, and laid it down under the wing of the Harrier, The Cubans—because I've found out where they're from by talking a little to Rosaria—are on the other side, near where the track begins. So, in the privacy of our warplane, Rosaria and I are as alone in this place as it's

160

possible to be.

She took one look at my domestic arrangements and said: 'If you touch me I'll kill you.'

I don't wish to be killed at this point, having survived so far, so I promised her she was safe. She fell asleep like a child, cuddling up to me with her thumb in her mouth.

My principal decision is whether or not to try to escape. I think for the moment I'll stay put, because although I'm in trouble here I'd be in more trouble on my own in the jungle with this lot chasing me. I wouldn't know which way to run. So long as I'm with the Harrier I know that the RAF at least will be looking for me.

And there's another thing. I keep ironicaly feeling I ought to stay here and keep an eye on the plane. It's a sense of ownership, or custodianship for the British taxpayer. I keep thinking of the fifteen million quid this plane costs to replace.

I'd just finished writing the above when a couple of fast jets went over, very low. The Cubans cursed, and waved their rifles. I felt very cheery. Good-night.

*　　*　　*

May 20.
No sign of Luis, which is not something that affects me directly, but which has put everyone
161

else here on edge. All morning Mendoza was pacing to and fro, and had several loud arguments with the others. Juan, the young hothead, apparently wanted to go off and find Luis on foot, but the others restrained him. Pity, I was all for Juan going out of my life, and perhaps being eaten by a crocodile.

Rosaria seems concerned about Luis, which has made me wonder again about their relationship. She said he was a friend of her father's, but I can't believe that's all there is to it. I'm not stupid: he was probably screwing her, but what I can't understand is what she sees in him. He must be twenty years older than her. None of my concern, anyway.

RAF jets again flew past in the area, but I couldn't see them from where we are. They sounded quite a long way away.

I can't help wondering what is going on in the outside world. The fact that the RAF is flying obviously means that the murders have been discovered. Therefore, those jets are presumably Harriers from the SMA, or, more likely, from other dispersal sites. I can imagine what the mood must be like there at the moment, and I wish I was there to feel it.

But the RAF overflying a foreign country is one thing; there must be more going on. That would depend on the motives of the people I'm with. Presumably no one saw this coming. Clearly not in Britain, but in Delmira or El

Libertador there must have been a hint something was going to happen. I wish I'd done more homework before I got here! El Libertador has territorial claims on Delmira; the junta has problems at home with armed guerrillas—probably backed by these jokers—and so the junta would have everything to gain by starting a fight with Britain or Delmira.

Except these people aren't on the government side.

Unless I'm *really* reading the situation wrong. How Machiavellian are politics in Central America? Would the junta stage this just to start a war?

Probably not. But I remember reading somewhere how the coup in El Libertador had been engineered by the CIA, and that the junta is propped up by them now. That's the sort of thing you take for granted, these days. But would the Americans stage something like this? I don't get it.

(Later.) We had a big visit this afternoon: a truck appeared at the top of the slope. I assumed immediately it was Luis, but this was a smaller vehicle, an ordinary lorry. There were a lot of people on board: all men, and all of them armed. One of them was obviously some kind of boss: much fraternal hugging and back-slapping went on, like Arabs or Frenchmen.

The Harrier was the star attraction, and I was the support. The boss was taken on a tour of the aircraft (he walked around it half a dozen times, in other words), and I was prodded forward at the point of three guns to stand in front of him. I felt strangely neutral. I suppose I should have been jut-jawed and defiant, and I suppose they would have preferred me to have been grovelling for mercy, but in actual fact I felt detached and irrelevant to the proceedings.

They wanted to photograph me, in g-suit and bone-dome, in front of the Harrier, and although I resisted at first, in the end I gave in. Being walloped on the side of the head with the butt of a rifle is quite a persuasive experience, I discovered.

I decided that it was time I looked defiant, but when the Polaroids were passed around I looked simply sulky. They took more, and I pulled the same face. I had an aching head for two hours after the blow, and my jaw felt sprained. Still does.

Good news: they took Juan away with them. Bad news: they left three more men in his place. Mendoza is still here, and still apparently in charge of the six other men.

Before the boss left, I was in for one more nasty moment. They had brought on the truck with them several huge tanks of what turned out to be aviation spirit. These were off-loaded from the truck with great difficulty, together with a diesel-powered pump

Mendoza came up to me, and told me to

refuel the Harrier. I had a sudden, crazed and whirling image of my having to fuel the plane up and take the boss for a joyride, and then I found I was shaking my head and backing away. Mendoza misunderstood, thought I was refusing. The rifle came up, but now I'm more scared of being hit with it than being shot by it, and so I backed off even further.

I told him I couldn't do it, told him I needed a ground-crew, told him it was the wrong kind of fuel . . . anything.

In the end he changed his mind very quickly. This puzzled me.

Before the truck left the fuel was dumped by the Harrier, right next to where I'd been sleeping. If this lot think I'm going to sleep here tonight, the way they chain-smoke, they're bloody wrong. With Rosaria's help, I pulled up some more long grass and made a new bivouac under the trees, quite a long way from the other men. No one stopped us.

In the end, after more bear-hugs, the truck left. What those photographs are going to be used for I can well imagine, but at least it means they have a vested interest in keeping me alive.

Before all this I'd heard those theories about the way hostages are supposed to develop psychological dependence on their captors. In my case it's just not true. If anything, the more I know of them, the less interest I have in them. I feel that they, ironically, are like me: minor pieces in a bigger game, one whose moves are being made over our heads. My main job is stay alive and stay fit, and be ready for action as soon as something is done to rescue me.

Settling down with Rosaria in our new bivouac I started to feel randy, and acted accordingly. She's a maddening girl: she alternately shows no self-consciousness about her body (stripping off in front of me to wash, etc.) and a terrific prudishness. So as she snuggled up against me I responded in kind, but Rosaria acted as if I had tried to rape her. She said she was a virgin, and told me to leave her alone.

Did as requested.

* * *

May 21.
Two more visits today: more photographs and strutting around. Obviously, the theft of this Harrier is a major event.

All this has given me cause to think about what might be going on, and I must admit I find my own conclusions alarming.

To start at the beginning, I've always interpreted the events of the world since 1945 as a struggle between the two superpowers and their allies, played out in the non-aligned or Third World countries. In other words, Russia and America have never actually declared war on each other, but have been fighting a war for nearly forty years.

The interesting thing about this is the way in which it has taken a number of different forms. Technology is at the heart of it, and the principal influence on the conduct of second-hand wars is the degree to which arms have been supplied.

The Vietnam war is unique, in that it was won by the technologically inferior side. The Americans had air-power, chemical weapons, almost endless resources, but a determined guerrilla army eventually succeeded.

The conflict in the Middle East would end within a matter of weeks if the superpowers cut off arms supplies. And yet ... the Irish republicans have successfully fought a war against the British for fifteen years without formal weapons supply; another instance of a technologically inferior force fighting a more or less even war with a military power. The irony of the Falklands war was that the Argentines were armed with British, European and American weapons, so that, for example, British ships were dodging French missiles, and that British-built Canberra bombers were being shot down by British-operated American missile systems, while French-built Argentine Mirage aircraft were dropping American-built bombs on British ships identical to ones they owned themselves.

But the point I'm getting round to is the subject of air-power. A determined guerrilla force has in the end the means to defeat a major power. Throughout the Vietnam war the Americans had total air superiority, threatened only by ground-based missiles.

If the Viet-Cong and the North Vietnamese had had an air force, how differently would the war have been fought? If the Palestinians had an air force, what would happen? If the IRA had aircraft...?

Now, what is interesting is that the RAF, as explained to me, is actively pursuing the policy of a guerrilla air force, one that is dispersed to hidden but almost completely independent bases, ones which are *intended* to survive pre-emptive enemy strikes and to continue fighting after more conventional forces have been immobilized.

The only thing that makes this possible is the Harrier jump-jet.

The plane still requires a highly-trained pilot, and still requires the support of a ground-crew. It would need a reliable supply of spares, fuel and ammunition ... but presuming that these things are always available on the arms black market, it is not beyond the bounds of belief that groups other than air forces could operate a Harrier.

It is, in fact, almost as if the Harrier were designed with field-operations in mind.

And I think it is my luck to be in on the first attempt to build a guerrilla air force.

When I first realized this, my blood ran cold. My position is still ambiguous. Are they expecting me to fly the thing?

I've thought about this almost incessantly from the time I was brought here. The real problem is that I can't fathom their way of thinking. Mendoza, in particular, seems erratic. But I think that if I really *were* a Harrier pilot— in other words, a serving officer in the RAF— and they were holding me captive, would they realistically expect me to go over to their side?

I think on balance they would not ... but that doesn't mean they might not try to make me.

But supposing that they would not, then it must mean that I am being held here as a hostage. They want something more, something they haven't already got.

Presumably this would be a real pilot, someone who could and would fly on their side. But where would they find one of those? The RAF is probably the least likely source in the world. I know we've sold Harriers to other countries—Spain, India, the United States—so there are other sources. But knowing what I know of the RAF flyers, air force pilots tend to be a dedicated breed, living and breathing their lives as pilots, the sort of men who are loyal without question. This would be as true of an

169

Indian or Spanish pilot as it is of one from Britain.

A commercial pilot? But the Harrier has always been exclusively a warplane.

(*Later.*) I was writing the above while the visitors were still here, but was interrupted by their departure. As soon as they had gone, Mendoza came over and tossed a rolled-up newspaper at me.

I'm headline news in Prudencia!

The picture of me standing in front of the Harrier covered half the front page, and an excited headline and article the rest of it. The headline said: HARRIER HOSTAGE.

It took me a while to read the article, and longer to get any sense from it. To get the truth I had to filter out at least three layers of confusion. (a) It was written in Spanish, a language I get by in. (b) The newspaper had all the hallmarks of being at least run by, and probably censored by, the government, and the source of much of the story would have come indirectly from these people, the forces who opposed the government. And (c) the journalistic style was sensationalist.

Even so, it was the first newspaper I'd seen in some days, and so I read it eagerly.

The sense of it was that the 'Cuban-backed terrorist organization', Los Enfadados, had released the above picture which claimed to show the captured British plane and the

170

kidnapped pilot. Demands had been made on the military junta who ran the country, and although these demands weren't spelt out, from reading between the lines I could guess it was the release of political detainees plus other concessions. Government forces were meanwhile moving in on 'rebel-held' territory, and several 'terrorist hide-outs' had been destroyed.

My heart sank when I read this, because recent history had shown that when 'government forces' went out in search of 'rebels' it was always women and children who got killed, and when 'hide-outs' were destroyed it usually meant schools, hospitals and houses had been hit.

Troublemakers and spies were being rounded up in Prudencia, which I knew meant that life was being made unpleasant for journalists.

Except: the newspaper repeated the familiar territorial claim on Delmira.

As I sat there looking at the unpleasant news, all I could think was the sooner these rebels and their government got together to pursue their claim on Delmira, the better. Then at least we British could move in and do something.

But then I repented of the thought. That way wars began, and if a war did begin, a lot more innocent people would be hurt.

But the news also had an immediacy for myself. If the government forces really *were* searching for us, I would have to face the possibility that one day they might find us here in our quarry. What might happen then, when under-trained soldiers appeared at the top of the quarry, was anybody's guess.

All in all, I am beginning to bank on the RAF's expertise at finding needles in haystacks.

CHAPTER SEVENTEEN

What happened to Luis Guedes was that he was arrested. It was all very mysterious, not least to Luis ... although he had sufficient complicity in the taking of the Harrier to feel guilty.

Luis fell into the hands of a group of the militia known, very simply, as the *Guardia Callado*: the Silent Police. These had been set up in the days of the dictator Limonta. Their primary allegiance was to themselves, to the secrecy of their operations, to the nature of their operations; technically, they were answerable to the junta. Their political coloration was of the right; so committed were they to an annexation of Delmira that they did not even consider there to be a frontier in force. The *Guardia Callado* had a ceremonial uniform, but it was not considered that their normal work was at all ceremonial. They were recognized, as it were, by the vacuum they created. If someone was snatched from his bed at four in the morning, it was the Callados. If there was gunfire in the streets, it was the Callados. If a family disappeared, it was the Callados. Their power was based on fear, and thus it was an immense power.

Luis knew all this, as everyone in his country knew this, but he did not realize it at the time it happened.

He had followed Mendoza's directions, and found the way down to the mountain road, and he was heading for the nearest diesel filling station he knew of: on the Guatemalan Highway, some fifty kilometres away.

Luis, an uncomplicated man, was intending to do what he had promised to do: refill the transporter's tanks and return to the hideout. His motive for doing this was exactly as he had described to Mendoza; duplicity was not in his soul. And he would indeed return. He had left the girl Rosaria as his voucher of reliability, and the small magic she had brought into his life was one he fully intended to sample again.

But on the highway he was stopped by an unmarked car, and the two middle-aged, humourless men who questioned him made it clear that his intentions were thwarted. From now his fate was theirs.

Luis believed they were *Policia*, as they told him, because that was what he wanted to believe. The words *Guardia Callado* did not

173

enter his mind, because they evoked such fright that he could not even contemplate them.

While they questioned him, a convoy of troop-carriers rattled past on the highway, but Luis was too preoccupied with his own troubles to notice.

They did not question him long. Soon he was in their car, and the transporter stood on the side of the highway as they accelerated away. Luis by now knew better than to ask what was happening. He waited dumbly for his fate.

This turned out to be a deserted wooden shack, windowless and doorless and running with rats. The two Guardia took him inside, and proceeded to ask for the information they required: where he had been, what he had been doing, who he had been with, and so on. They knew what the transporter was used for, and they had a shrewd idea what it had just been doing.

Luis, thinking of Rosaria, said nothing. He had very little to say after the first hour, and at the end of the second hour a bullet between the eyes made sure that he never said anything again.

What the motives for these two Guardia might have been can only be guessed at, because Luis' body was then taken back in the car to the transporter; it was dumped in the driver's seat behind the wheel, and the transporter was set alight.

By the time Luis' body was recovered from the smouldering wreckage, considerable burns had disfigured his face and body, but he was soon accurately identified and the civil police discovered the actual cause of his death. It did not raise many suspicions, as mysterious suicides were commonplace in El Libertador in those days.

*   *   *

What happened to José Nicolás was that he began to have doubts.

It began almost as soon as he found himself accepted into the resistance cause. The one quality that distinguished José was the independence of his mind, the ability, consciously exercised, of judging issues on their merits without external influence. He did not rush into such judgements. It was this independence which had made clear to him the phonyness of his role in Prudencia. He had grown suspicious of the American presence there, and then angry. At the same time, his own discoveries in the city and countryside had made clear to him the facts of life in modern El Libertador. The ordinary people were being oppressed and exploited. On the one side they were being oppressed by a corrupt and self-serving regime, which was in time-honoured fashion creaming off the wealth of the country into their own pockets, and letting the masses fend for themselves. There was no rightness there, and yet it was a system being propped up by the United States, the country he had loved and the one that had become his home.

But equally were the people being exploited by the guerrillas. Their weakness made them open to manipulation, and although their sense of grievance against the junta was genuine enough, and Los Enfadados had begun as a force of real freedom fighters, when the Cubans saw an opportunity to manipulate instability, there was no means of halting them.

At first, José's induction into the rebel cause went well.

He was shown clear and unarguable evidence of what the junta was planning.

First, his own role in El Libertador. He had been told that the government was re-equipping with Northrop F-5E Tigers. The Tiger was a plane José had flown and was familiar with. It was above all a fast combat jet, the sort of plane many countries were equipping with as a defence against external threats. José had no political opinions on such matters; he was a flyer, and he could teach flying.

But this was not true. The junta was in the process of negotiating the purchase of about fifty ex-Marines AV-8As, the US version of the Harrier.

Like the Tiger, the Harrier could certainly be

used as a front-line defence combat aircraft, but it was so flexible it could be put to almost any use.

The rebels pointed out to José that almost the entire air force in El Libertador to date consisted of Cessna A-37Bs, planes *designed* for counter-insurgency operations. Regimes throughout Latin America were equipping with such aircraft. Another was the Argentine-built IA-58 Pucará, used to deadly effect in the Falklands war. Yet another was the Fairchild A-10A Thunderbolt, possibly the most destructive ground-aircraft ever built.

All these planes were similar in that they were cheap to buy and maintain, they were purpose-built for the job, and because of their design simplicity they were dangerous to their victims but also virtually undamageable to those inside them.

The El Libertador Cessnas were getting old and were due for replacement. Thunderbolts had been seriously considered, but in the end the coming availability of secondhand American Harriers had proved too tempting. With one or perhaps two squadrons of these, the junta would have not only a front-line combat force the envy of every other country in Latin America, but would have a counter-insurgency force that would effectively maintain and increase the level of oppression for as long ahead as anyone could see.

But secondly, José was shown direct evidence
of the cruelty of the regime. He met a woman
whose breasts had been removed with a knife;
the man whose genitals had been pierced with a
white-hot needle; the children whose parents
had vanished off the face of the earth; a twenty-
five-year-old woman whose hair was
prematurely grey as a result of electro-shock
torture. He was taken to shops that had been
burned out, to walls pock-marked with bullet-
holes from the executions that had taken place,
to a railway siding where four carriages of a
freight-train had been found to be crammed
with bodies of young men.

It appalled him and it gave him a cause, and
to José Nicolás there was no doubt that what he
was being shown was true. He felt that his
American background had instilled in him a
pure sense of fairness and/ rightness, that
wrongness was an absolute. Until he returned to
El Libertador he had never had the facts with
which to test such a moral principle.

But above all he still had what some might
describe as the curse of free-thinking. He
accepted what he was shown, but he never
believed for one moment that it represented the
whole.

Nevertheless, he had made an irreversible
decision in joining the rebels. He had deserted
his country, betrayed his fellow Marines, and
José knew that from now on all his actions had

to support this commitment. He earnestly sought support for his actions. The junta had to be overthrown; the people of the country had to be given the rights and freedoms of democracy.

This struggle had been going on a long time before José turned up in Prudencia, and its methods had become long established.

While he was actually there, living in the squalid Prudencian back streets, the freedom fighters of Los Enfadados, as backed by the Cubans, committed a number of revolutionary acts.

There was a machine-gun attack on a police station. Three officers inside were killed, and seven passers-by.

A car bomb exploded near the Presidential Palace. Seventeen people died, none of them belonging to government forces.

The Roman Catholic cathedral was occupied by gunmen, claiming to liberate it for the people. They were killed in a gun-battle, which also claimed the lives of two Guardia officers and five civilian hostages.

The wife of a government minister was found dead. She had been raped, and her throat had been cut.

A group of five- and six-year-old children were taken hostage in a government-run private school on the outskirts of Prudencia. None of them was hurt, but they were held prisoner for two days. Both gunmen were later arrested, and had since disappeared.

This was how it happened that José Nicolás began to have doubts.

★　　★　　★

HMS *Invincible* was cruising in international waters, just below the horizon to the west of Prudencia City. Everyone in the world knew she was there, and why she was there. In the Security Council of the UN, the British Ambassador to the UN had made Britain's demands quite plain: the Harrier was to be returned to the RAF, the journalist held hostage was to be released, and the men who had murdered the RAF ground-crew were to be extradited to Delmira. Additionally, Britain asked for full recognition of Delmira as an independent country by the El Libertador regime.

None of these demands were being met, so to step up the pressure the two British aircraft-carriers now in the region, together with the RAF based in Delmira, were regularly penetrating El Libertadorense air-space. There were a lot of Harriers in that area.

One of the more sinister side-effects of the Falklands war had been the boom in sales of anti-ship missiles, the brand leader of course being the French-built Exocet. Indeed, Exocets were the new status-symbol of the Third World.

180

El Libertador had its armoury of Exocets, and had been looking for an excuse to fire a few of them off. Practice firing was expensive, and not the same thing at all.

The presence of *Invincible* so close to El Libertador was a temptation it would have needed Hercules to resist. The junta did not consist of Herculean minds.

Two ground-based Exocet C-2 missiles were duly launched in the specific direction of the British carrier, while the junta, as it were, stood on the parapets of the palace and watched with interested eyes.

The British, however, are a unique race, and one of the many reasons for that uniqueness is that the British are one of the very, very few peoples on this planet to have had an Exocet missile fired at them in anger.

The British do not like having Exocets fired at them.

The two Exocets the Libertadorense regime fired at the *Invincible* did not, as the saying goes, hit.

What happened to the two Exocets was that they were intercepted in mid-flight by extremely sophisticated, and highly top secret, defensive systems. Another reason for British uniqueness is that the British have learned how to shoot down Exocets.

The regime fired two more, doubling the original crime.

The British dealt with the second two as efficiently as they had dealt with the first two, but they liked those missiles and the people who had fired them even less.

No more Exocets were fired at *Invincible*.

Instead, *Invincible* launched a few Harriers in anger.

Meanwhile, on the plains of Delmira, the RAF, who in spite of inter-service rivalry actually felt extremely loyal to their colleagues in the Royal Navy, sent some Harriers on a sortie to Prudencia too.

Events were drawing towards a climax.

CHAPTER EIGHTEEN

On the same morning that Exocets were fired at *Invincible*, John Wolfe woke up in the humid and flower-perfumed quarry, the girl Rosaria lying in his arms. His back and neck were aching from sleeping rough, and the weight of the girl's arm across his chest only added to his discomfort. But in the night he had discovered Rosaria's virginal way of love-making, and the consequent sense of physical release lent a feeling of normality.

He roused, and moved the girl to one side. The sun was already up, and across the stony floor of the quarry Wolfe could see the Cubans.

Most of the group were sitting tensely about the front of the truck, but one of them was away to the side, pissing against a tree.

Wolfe ignored them, and went down to the shallow, stagnant pool to splash the warm water over his face, neck and chest.

He got some food from the Cubans, but they were all nervy and jumpy, and Wolfe moved away from them. He sat in the shadow of the Harrier's wing and spooned up the spicy slop they had given him. His stomach was at long last adjusting to the local food, but he liked the taste no more than he had ever done.

The reason for the Cuban's jumpy state soon became clear. A dark green Land Rover appeared at the top of the quarry track, causing the Cubans to take up their rifles and sprawl into hurriedly chosen defensive positions. The arrival was clearly both expected and unexpected, as if they had known someone was due to arrive, but not who it would be or when.

The Land Rover halted, and the slim figure of a young man appeared. In the now familiar surroundings of the quarry, he made an odd figure because he was wearing a flyer's g-suit and sunglasses. At once the Cubans relaxed, and waved up to him. The young man got back into the Land Rover, and drove carefully down to them.

Wolfe had drawn back under the broad wing of the Harrier, Rosaria beside him, but

183

something about the confident manner of the
new arrival gave him a sense of reassurance.

The driver of the Land Rover stopped the
vehicle, and was greeted by Mendoza and the
others. This time, there was none of the
comradely bear-hugging of before. It was clear
that this was a different calibre of man, bringing
a new pattern of authority. While talking to the
Cubans, he kept glancing towards the Harrier,
and then at last Mendoza said something,
pointing specifically at John Wolfe.

At once, the young man left them and walked
quickly over, managing to appraise both Wolfe
and the aircraft. He stuck out his hand.

'I guess you must be John Wolfe,' he said, in
a pleasant American accent. 'Good to meet you.
I'm Joe Nicholas.'

'Who are you?' Wolfe said suspiciously.

'Well, you could say I'm the new pilot around
here. What I want to know is, are you a pilot or
aren't you?'

Wolfe, having spent much time considering
this, said: 'I'm a journalist, but I've flown as
navigator.'

'Okay, Mr Wolfe.' Nicholas looked back to
where Mendoza stood. 'Now I've got a
proposition to put to you, and I'd like you to
make up your mind damned fast. I'm going to
fly this bird, and I can fly it with or without
your help. If you help me, it means I can get my
job done just that little bit easier and faster; if

you don't help me, I guess I'm going to have to let Mr Mendoza dispose of you.'

'You're not giving me much choice.'

'I'm not intending to.'

After several days stagnating in this place, Wolfe realized he was not going to get out alive the way things were going. If he flew with Nicholas, whatever their destination, there was more of a chance he'd get out.

'What do you want me to do?' he said.

'Well, the first thing is to figure out how to fuel this baby up. What do you say?'

'Okay.' Nicholas looked steadily at him.

They had spoken English throughout this, with Mendoza looking uncomprehendingly from one to the other.

'You're an American?' Wolfe said.

'That's right. So what?'

'So . . . what are you doing with this lot?'

'I'm a flyer of warplanes, Mr Wolfe. That's my employment, and I'm employed to fly warplanes for these people.'

Nicholas said this defiantly, but also defensively, a note of uncertainty that Wolfe could not help but note.

With the arrival of Nicholas in the hideout, it was clear who was now running the place. Mendoza and his men were given the job of levelling the ground in front of the jet fighter, and removing as much of the loose soil and small rocks as possible. By chance, Luis had

185

deposited the aircraft in a place where a short roll-forward and a vertical ascent would be possible.

Nicholas went about his preparations quickly and professionally. He first went underneath the aircraft, and located the refuelling points. He showed Wolfe how to connect up the pump, and start loading fuel aboard. While Wolfe got on with this, feeling his hands were clumsy and his arms weak, Nicholas scrambled up into the front cockpit and with some difficulty eased himself down into the seat.

Standing right next to the fuselage, Wolfe could hear the American say, 'Wow!' and 'Gee!' but in a quiet, appreciative way.

'What's up?' Wolfe said in the end, his curiosity aroused.

'You Brits sure have different planes from ours. It seems to me half the instruments are missing, and replaced with a whole bunch more.'

'Want me to show you what's what?' Wolfe said, suddenly feeling self-confident, out of all proportion to reality.

'I can figure it out. It's basically the same plane.'

Afterwards, Nicholas scrambled back to the rear cockpit, and took a note of what was there. Later, he went underwing, and checked out the weapons systems.

'Okay,' he said to Wolfe at the end of all this.

'Our big problem is ammunition, because we can't replace it right now. What we've got on the plane is all we've got. But the cannon is fully operational, we have a pod of Matra rockets, which makes me feel good, four Sidewinders, which makes me feel even better, and a couple of bombs, which I don't give a damn about. They might come in useful.'

Wolfe said: 'Are we going on a mission?'

'Right.'

'Today . . . I mean, now?'

'In a while.'

Nicholas wandered off, and spoke briefly to Mendoza. The Cuban nodded, then said something to the other men. Nicholas went to the Land Rover, and reached inside.

Rosaria had watched all this from the place where she and Wolfe had been sleeping, but now she walked over to him and held his arm.

'Don't leave me with these bastards,' she said in Spanish.

'I don't have any choice.'

'Then I'm coming with you. I'm scared.'

'I'm going in the Harrier. There's no way you can come. You'll have to stay.'

'No!' Tears welled in her eyes, and Wolfe felt a panicky sense of pity for her. He didn't want to think what might happen to her after he had left. He looked around the small area, wondering what to suggest.

In the end, grasping at a straw, he said:

'Rosaria, can you drive a car?'

'I think so.'

'Can you or can't you?'

'Yes. I drove for my father once.'

'All right. When I've gone, in the jet, I don't know what will be happening here ... but if you get a chance, take the Land Rover. I'll make sure the key is still in it. You know your way up the track? Just get in and drive like hell.'

'Yes.'

But her voice betrayed uncertainty. Wolfe said: 'Or just run. Get to the top of the quarry ... there's sure to be a track, because all these lorries have been coming here the last few days. You'll find a way.'

'You and I escape together.'

'They're watching me,' Wolfe said. 'You know that as well as I do. But when the jet takes off there'll be a lot of noise, and you could run then.'

'You don't want me,' she said, clinging more tightly to him.

'I want you, Rosaria,' he said. 'But it's not possible now.'

Nicholas was returning from the Land Rover, and he had under his arm a shining bone-dome helmet, painted with red white and blue stripes.

'Okay, Wolfe ... let's get the show on the road. I got work to do.'

'Is the plane ready?'

'If it isn't we're about to find out.' Nicholas

saw Wolfe's expression, and added: 'Listen, the plane's new to me. It's the same basic model as the one I'm used to, but it's a different machine. In addition, I got to take off vertically from an unprepared site, and fly without maps. That's all the bad news. The good news is I'm trained for jobs like this, and I love flying and I'm good at it. All you gotta do is sit in the cockpit at the back and do what I tell you. You got that?'

'Yes.' John Wolfe followed the young American to the aircraft, stopping off on the way to pick up his own, bullet-creased bone-dome. While they walked, he eased the helmet down snugly over his ears, but then took it off again, remembering the cockpit procedure.

He heard Nicholas telling Mendoza what to do. Basically, it was to keep out of the way, because stones and grit were going to be flying about. The best thing to do, he said, was to lie face-down and keep the ears covered.

Hearing this, Wolfe sidestepped quickly to Rosaria.

'Listen,' he said urgently. 'Do what I tell you. As soon as the plane takes off, use the noise as a cover. Get to the Land Rover.'

'But—'

'I'll come and see you again,' he lied. 'Just do what I tell you now, because otherwise you're going to be trapped here.'

She nodded dumbly. Wolfe squeezed her hand, then kissed her lightly and chastely on the lips. She turned away quickly, pretending to be angry, so while she had her back turned Wolfe walked on towards the Harrier. It had been so much a part of his life for the last few days, that it had come to seem a familiar size, but now, knowing as he did that it was about to fly again, it assumed more awesome proportions. The rocket-pod and the Sidewinder missiles looked dangerous, the plane looked like a killer. He felt the muscles above his knees start to tremble, and the palms of his hands felt sweaty.

Joe Nicholas was already almost in the front cockpit, one leg straddling the edge.

'You know how to hitch yourself in?' he said.

'Yes, I think so,' Wolfe said.

Nicholas disregarded him, and got on with his own settling in, so Wolfe clambered up to the rear-seat cockpit and feeling even more clumsy than the first time, lowered himself into the seat.

He tried to think of all the things that had been done. He remembered the pressure system for the g-suit, and got that connected up, and he remembered the oxygen supply. There was a survival kit somewhere, and after a moment of hunting around he located it down beside his legs on the left-hand side. This too he connected to his suit. He got his legs into the restrainers, then started fidgeting uncomfortably in an attempt to strap himself in.

He discovered why there was usually a

ground-crewman to assist the air-crew in these
pre-flight precautions. In front of him, he could
see Joe Nicholas having the same difficulties.
They both struggled to wrap the straps around
them, for over ten minutes, at the end of which
Wolfe was sweating uncomfortably in his g-suit.
At last he managed it, clunking the buckle tight
over his stomach, then pulling and twisting to
tighten the straps' hold on him.

'How're you doing?' Nicholas shouted from
in front of him.

'I'm about finished.'

'Okay ... then get your helmet on, and we
can talk without shouting.'

Wolfe did as he had been told, and plugged in
the oxygen and radiophone leads.

'All right, Wolfe, I want you to listen
carefully. I'm going to start the engine in a
minute, and once I do you're not to do anything
unless I tell you, and you're definitely not to say
anything. I'm going to have a lot on my mind.
You got that?'

'Yes. What's going to happen?'

'Okay, you know how to use the ejector seat?
You can't use it until I arm it, and when I arm it
I'll tell you to use it. Don't delay. Just get the
hell out of here.'

'All right,' Wolfe said, remembering that
Dave Hartford had made much the same sort of
comment just before they took off.

'Once we're flying, we're going to observe

191

total radio silence. I can talk to you, but we won't be talking to anyone outside, and we won't be listening either. Whatever happens outside, I mean *whatever*, we do whatever we want, we answer to nobody, and if we get into any kind of trouble I'm going to shoot my way out of it. Okay?'

'Okay,' Wolfe said, more nervously.

'Right, now I'll tell you our flight-plan. Once we get in the air, the first job is to locate this site visually, so we can find out way back.'

'We're coming *back*?'

'Yeah, what did you think? This isn't a one-off flight, you know. We're fighting a war.'

Wolfe's heart sank at the thought of returning to this hide-out. Somehow he had imagined that once he and Nicholas were in the air everything would change, and he would be free. He knew nothing about the war they wanted to fight: his only wish was to get back to Delmira. And thence, home.

'Once we've located this place, we're going on a little visit to Prudencia. We got a few surprises for them.'

Wolfe said nothing.

'Did you hear that, Wolfe?'

'Yes, I heard. Captain Nicholas, what the hell are you doing this for?'

'I told you, I'm a flyer.'

'You were flying for the US Marines. Don't you see how crazy all this is?'

There was a long silence, and Wolfe saw the striped bone-dome helmet tip forward slightly, as if the man was thinking.

'I've got a score to settle, on behalf of my people here.'

'All right. But then what?'

'I've made a decision, and I'm committed to it.'

'You mean you betrayed your country.'

Another long silence. Then: 'I've returned to my own country.'

'This God-awful shit-hole? You prefer this to the United States?'

'I've made my decision,' Nicholas said again.

'You've made a bloody awful decision. It's not too late.'

'You mean, go back?'

'That's exactly what I mean.'

'I walked out on my buddies in Prudencia. That's the decision I made.'

'You mean there are other American pilots here?' Wolfe said.

'Eight in all.'

Wolfe thought quickly. A small detachment of American pilots in a foreign country meant only one thing: a CIA operation. But since the early 1980s the Central Intelligence Agency, against its own wishes, had been made more and more answerable to the elected representatives in Washington DC. The sort of undercover operation that had engineered the overthrow of

Allende in Chile was now strictly illegal, which didn't mean, of course, that it was now impossible.

'You were attached to the embassy?'

'No. Now can it, Wolfe. We got a job of work to do.'

There was a whining noise from behind Wolfe, and after a moment of dying hesitation, the engine fired. A familiar vibration coursed through him. Wolfe glanced to the side, and saw that Mendoza and his men, who all through their preparations had been standing in a loose semi-circle around the aircraft, were now backing away, covering their ears with their hands.

The canopy slid down from behind, cutting out much of the noise. Wolfe looked across the clearing, and saw the white-bloused figure of Rosaria. By some miracle, apparently, she had actually listened to what he said, and had moved round to a position not far from the Land Rover.

'Listen to me, Wolfe. This operation's going ahead, and while it does I want no talk-back from you. You got that? Life's gonna get pretty dangerous in the next few minutes.'

'All right. But I think you can change your mind. You've done nothing wrong.'

'Shut up, Wolfe. I want a fuel-reading from you, and when I tell you, I want the weapons systems armed.'

'Fuel, number one tank, 98% capacity, and running.'

'Okay. Let's get going.'

The engine noise increased, and the plane moved forward slowly from under the trees. Looking to the side, Wolfe saw Mendoza and his men still backing away, their hands clasped violently over their ears. The trees and bushes were waving frantically in the jet stream, and a storm of dust, pebbles and gravel skittered over the ground. One by one, the men threw themselves on the ground. Beyond them, still just out of the range of impact from the aircraft's exhaust, Rosaria was moving towards the Land Rover.

The plane halted, but the engine-noise mounted, and suddenly there was a groaning and shaking, the wings wobbled slightly ... and Wolfe realized that they had started their lift-off. Now the debris from the jet-stream was rising darkly around them, but the Harrier was lifting steadily, with just the slightest wobbling of the nose and wings to convey the pilot's unfamiliarity with the craft. The walls of the quarry were slipping down beneath them, and Wolfe could no longer see anything of the people below them. Whether or not Rosaria got safely to the Land Rover he did not see. The engine noise was still mounting, and the plane was beginning to move forward in the air. Wolfe felt the familiar press of acceleration, the clunk

195

of the undercarriage recovering to its housing. The Harrier was becoming a conventional fast jet.

The quarry was now visible as a scar in the forest, marked by two yellow-coloured tracks through the trees. Nicholas circled the area twice, shouting through the intercom to Wolfe to mark local landmarks: the tracks, the curve of a river, an outcrop of rocks. It all looked readily identifiable while they were close to it, but as soon as they started moving away it was all less clear.

Then the Harrier dived towards the forest, picking up speed, starting its low-level run towards the capital city a hundred miles to the west.

CHAPTER NINETEEN

The total British strength of the air-strike against the Libertadorense mainland was eight Harriers. There were four from *Invincible*, leaving one Sea Harrier in reserve, and four from the RAF dispersal sites inside Delmira. One of the RAF Harriers was kept in reserve.

The four Sea Harriers attacked the known sites of the Exocet ground-based launchers; one was completely destroyed, and the other was damaged to the point where it would not be operational again for some weeks. In one of the attacks there was an immense underground explosion—whose blast-effects could be clearly seen on the film taken of the action—and from this it was presumed that an ammunition dump had received a direct hit.

Armed port installations in Prudencia Harbour were attacked a few minutes later, and several hits were claimed. Several boats in the harbour were destroyed, including a small ocean-going yacht called the *Saigon*.

Meanwhile, the RAF Harriers were attacking government bases inland.

Both the international civilian airport and the military air base were attacked. The civilian airport had to have its runways cratered, to prevent its use by the military; this operation was completely successful, in that the military aims were achieved without a single civilian life being lost. At the air-base, the Harriers met concentrated anti-aircraft fire, but succeeded in destroying nine Cessna A-37Bs on the ground, and damaging several more. No aircraft was sent up to challenge them, and the main runway was damaged.

Two of the Harriers sustained damage, but remained operational. For the remainder of their operating time, the four RAF Harriers deployed in low-level fast passes over the centre of Prudencia, using noise hazard and sonic booms as anti-morale devices. The civilian population of Prudencia were left in no doubt that the British wanted their stolen Harrier back.

However, confusion operates without frontiers. None of the eight British pilots involved in the raids was aware that flying amongst them, conducting a raid of its own, was the very Harrier that all the trouble was about.

★   ★   ★

As they approached the city, Joe Nicholas said down the intercom: 'There's something going on!'

He pointed dead ahead, and Wolfe, squinting in the bright daylight was just able to pick out the dark silhouette of a small jet scudding over the rooftops. In the distance, columns of smoke were rising, bending with the wind. Then another jet appeared, going the other way. Wolfe could see the sweep-back of its wings.

'Whose are they?' he shouted.

'I don't give a shit.'

Nicholas took the jet even lower, and started swinging from left to right to avoid any gunfire that might be aimed their way. The centre of the city approached, and two more jets shot past them.

'Harriers!' Nicholas said. 'Do you know anything about this?'

'No.'

One went by, then flipped over on its side and vanished. Wolfe just caught a glimpse of a silvery underside, the familiar roundel on an engine nacelle.

'They're Limeys. Sea Harriers! Is there a carrier here?'

'I don't know.'

They passed the centre of the city, went out over the sea, where more jets were operating. Nicholas threw the Harrier into a steep turn, forcing Wolfe down into his seat, his face distending with the terrific g-force on them. When the world steadied again they were on a straight track for the centre of the city once more.

A banging and throbbing passed through the aircraft, then Nicholas shouted. 'Arm the rockets!'

'I don't know how!'

'It's marked with an orange tab.'

Wolfe looked down at the panel in front of him, and saw, under a transparent plastic sheath, a row of four orange tabs. He knocked the sheath away, and tried to move the tabs, but they seemed locked in place.

'Hurry up, you bastard!' Nicholas shouted.

'They won't shift!'

They had passed the centre of the city, and were overflying what looked like cane plantations.

'Listen, Wolfe, we haven't much fuel left.

Those tabs *turn*, then drop down, okay?'

The plane banked steeply, and again the g-forces seemed to flatten them; the pressure was so great Wolfe could not raise his hands to the panel. When the plane straightened, and once again was heading for the centre of the city, he grabbed the tabs as he'd been told, and shot all four of them into the downward position.

'Right. Now fuel up-date!'

'Number one tank . . . Jesus! 4% capacity!'

'Go to tanks two and three, now!'

Wolfe found the control under the read-out, and turned the handle. At once the up-dated fuel supply stabilized near the 95% mark.

It was all happening too fast. The plane banged and juddered again, and this time Wolfe saw the cannon-fire shooting forward in white-hot flashes, seeming to drop down towards a large, painted building. A tremendous *whoosh*ing noise followed, and Wolfe felt a great heat radiating against his face. Rockets were blasting forth from their pod beneath the port wing, and scattering explosively across the roof of the palace. But then Nicholas banked away, climbing towards the blue sky, and g-forces pressed down. Another Harrier was crazily in sight for an instant, flashing blackly across the blazing sky, but Nicholas wrenched the plane away, the g-force squeezing like a press urging the last drop from a broken apple. Wolfe greyed out for a few moments, recovering his wits when the plane straightened and dived sharply towards the ground.

Hugging the contours it headed back to that part of the hilly forest where the rebels had made their hideout.

*　　*　　*

Later that day, when both the Fleet Air Arm and the RAF pilots had been debriefed, Britain issued a denial that the presidential palace had been attacked deliberately. All the pilots had been under strict orders to attack only military targets.

However, it was undeniable that a British Harrier *had* attacked the palace, and Britain therefore issued a stiff and evasively worded apology to the military rulers of El Libertador. They were, in fact, very sorry indeed that Brigadier-General Alejandro Vinet, one of the three-man junta, had been killed in the action.

CHAPTER TWENTY

Flying over the jungle, John Wolfe said: 'What next?'

'I told you not to speak. I'm busy.'

The striped helmet in front of him, turning from side to side, bobbing like a puppet's head to the instruments.

'What do we do next?'

'Fuel up-date! Come on, man!'

'Tanks two and three, 27% and running.'

'Have you put the weapons systems on safety?'

'No.'

'Jesus H.!'

Wolfe flicked the orange tabs upwards, and twisted them. The plastic sheath had fallen down somewhere beneath his knees.

'They're safe.'

'All right ... what we do next is find the hide-out, and land. Then we re-fuel, and go out again. We've still got rockets left, as well as the cannon.'

'Don't you see this is mad!'

'All war is mad ... or so they say.'

'Look, Nicholas, we weren't alone just then. The British are doing everything you want to do. They've got reserves of fuel and bombs ... what are we going to do when we run out of rockets?'

'Wait for more to come in. Now can it.'

'And what do you think these Cubans are going to achieve? A socialist state?'

No answer; the helmet bobbed from side to side, then the plane banked steeply.

'Whoever it was who brought you here was acting illegally. It was probably the CIA. Do you realize that?'

'It was the US Marine Corps, man.'

'You're fooling yourself. It was a crazy CIA operation, and you got out of it, and because of that you think you've betrayed your country.'

'What are you saying, Wolfe?'

'Throw in your lot with the British. No problem.'

'Shut up!'

The plane banked a second time, and a deep vibration announced that the engine was pulling back. Wolfe looked down to the side, and to his amazement saw a turn of river, a yellow track, a scar in the deep-green forest layer.

'How's the fuel?'

'14% and running.'

'Okay ... no need to go on reserve. Hold tight.'

The nose of the plane went up, a familiar wobble ran across the plane from side to side, and the engine note rose heavily. The Harrier began to descend. Wolfe looked down, his heart sinking at the thought of returning to imprisonment.

He found his legs and body were tense with the rigours of the landing, and he made himself relax. But the plane was moving awkwardly, sinking to the ground rather more quickly than Wolfe would have liked. The trees and shrubs started to move violently in the downthrust, and a vicious cloud of dust swept upwards.

On the ground, Mendoza's men were dashing

to the safety of the truck.

And where once it had been left, Wolfe noted that the Land Rover had disappeared. Then everything was lost to sight in the dust-storm thrown up by the engine.

The plane hit the ground, the nose bobbed, and then the engine whined down to silence.

'What was that you were saying, Wolfe?' The striped helmet moved from side to side, and the canopy hissed back.

*   *   *

An hour later, the plane had been refuelled and the remaining weapons checked. Captain Joe Nicholas was a hero, because one of Mendoza's men had a transistor radio, and a Prudencia station announced that British Harriers had raided the city and destroyed a number of installations as well as seriously damaging the presidential palace.

There were still four or five hours of daylight, and Nicholas was in discussions with Mendoza. On the ground, Wolfe's role reverted to hostage ... or refueller. He wandered around the quarry, feeling impotent and alarmed. How much longer could Joe Nicholas go on making raids against the government? It couldn't be long before this hideout was traced by somebody ... even the British. In that dashing, gut-turning raid on the palace, he had glimpsed enough of what was going on to realize a major sortie was taking place. The rebels thought it had all been done by Nicholas in the captured Harrier, but by a coincidence their visit to the capital had happened at the same time as a British air-raid.

But they certainly *had* hit the presidential palace good and hard.

He was missing Rosaria, in an odd way. None of the Cubans said anything about her, but it was safe to assume she had got away. There was no sign of the Land Rover at all . . . and he had looked as far up the track as he could see, dreading that he would see its bullet-riddled remains. But she appeared to have escaped completely.

Maybe, he thought ironically, he should have made her wait, and he could have taken the Land Rover with her . . .

Now he was as much a prisoner as before, and with no hope of escape.

A few minutes later, Nicholas came up to him.

'We're going to burn up the rockets we've got,' he said. 'Mendoza says that they can get more for us in a week or so, but that's too long to wait. I'm going to go in now, before sunset.'

He walked away towards the Harrier, and Wolfe followed, presuming he was included in the plans. He was tired after the first flight, and did not want to do another. But as had happened before, it presented a momentary illusion of escape.

Nicholas had started to climb up to the cockpit, and Wolfe was standing at the base of the aircraft, when five or six of the loudest explosions Wolfe had ever heard detonated about the quarry. He reeled round in terror, his head ringing with the noise. Yellow smoke was drifting thickly across the clearing, and through it there came a continuing chatter of small-arms fire.

Then there was silence, and into the silence there came a loudly amplified voice. It had a Birmingham accent.

It said: 'JOHN WOLFE! GET ON THE FOOCKING FLOOR!'

More explosions followed, and Wolfe threw himself on the ground. Someone dashed past, firing a sub-machine gun—from the hip.

Joe Nicholas thudded down to the ground beside Wolfe.

'What the hell . . .?'

'Keep your head down.'

Another man appeared, dressed in British Army combat gear. He looked down at the two men on the ground.

'Stay there!' he shouted, and dashed away. The smoke was clearing, but every now and then there would be another shattering explosion. The Cubans had found their rifles and were putting up a fight, but they didn't have a snowball's chance in hell. Squinting up from his prone position, Wolfe saw Mendoza running out from behind the truck, firing wildly at the British, but something hit him in the legs and he fell to the floor, doubled up and rolling over.

There were more shots, more sporadically. Wolfe raised his head.

The soldier re-appeared miraculously from the trees.

'Oi told you to keep your foocking head down,' he shouted, and went on. There was a silence, and a few more shots.

Then a new silence, and this one endured.

*   *   *

Mendoza, by some chance, had survived, although he was wounded in a horrible way across the legs and groin. He lay on the ground, moaning endlessly.

'Which one of you two's John Wolfe?'

'I am.'

'Are these the boogers who killed our lads?'

'Well, not all of them . . .'

'They're all dead, except this one.'

'That's Mendoza. I saw him shooting one of the ground-crew. He's a bastard.'

'Our orders are to extradite the men who killed our lads,' said the soldier. He turned to one of the others. 'Hey, Jimmy. You can extradite that one too.'

Wolfe closed his eyes, and turned away. When he looked back, Mendoza was dead.

'Now who's this?' the Birmingham soldier said to Wolfe, meaning Joe Nicholas.

Wolfe and Nicholas were still lying face-down on the ground.

Wolfe said: 'He's an American pilot.'

'What's a bloody Yank doing in this dump?'

Nicholas started to say something, but the soldier kicked him.

Wolfe said: 'The same as me. He's a hostage.'

'All right, you can both stand up.'

*   *   *

Later, the soldier said: 'You two are coming with us. We're going to have to dynamite the plane.'

'*Dynamite* it!' Wolfe said. 'Why?'

'Do you want us to leave it for these boogers?'

'For God's sake don't destroy it. We can fly it out of here.'

'You can't fly, Wolfe.'

'But he can. He's a Harrier pilot.'

'Okay, you fly it out.'

In the background the rest of the squad were tidying up: that is, they were loading whatever food, ammunition and arms they could find on to the truck, preparatory to driving it away. The bodies of the Cubans had been dragged under the trees.

★   ★   ★

Everyone was about to depart, and Wolfe said to the Brummie: 'Are you . . .? I mean, are you part of the—?'

'You didn't see us here, son. We're territorials, if you know what I mean. Training exercise. Don't ask stupid bloody questions.'

So Wolfe asked no more questions, being extremely impressed by the speed and efficiency of the raid, and distinctly apprehensive of what would happen if he crossed this squad of fifteen highly trained men.

From that point on, the squad paid no more attention to them, but finished loading the truck and checking it for booby-traps.

Meanwhile, John Wolfe and Joe Nicholas shook hands.

Wolfe said: 'No more discussions, right?'

Nicholas said: 'I'm sorry, man.'

'Sorry? What for?'

'For messing with you.'

They climbed back into the Harrier, and together went through their pre-flight checks. A few minutes later, as the army squad was preparing to leave, the Harrier lifted away from the quarry.

It turned towards the east, heading downwind to Delmira.

CHAPTER TWENTY-ONE

Sensing that bad news was about to break, Mr Charles D. Platten, of New York City, quickly had his bags packed, and headed for Prudencia's international airport.

It was estimated that it would take a week for the runways to be repaired, and so Mr Platten returned to his office in Prudencia. His staff were extremely annoyed that he had tried to walk out on them, and Mr Platten eventually apologized.

When he tried to call Washington DC, through the line patched into South-Western Bell, he was told the number was unobtainable. That not being so, for Mr Platten had been in the oil business long enough to know when he was being fobbed off, Mr Platten tried to make a connection through the regular El Libertador exchange. All trunk lines, he was informed, were down.

Later, he discovered that his telex machine had been sabotaged.

Later still, he discovered—to what was by now his acute annoyance—that the *Saigon* had been damaged beyond repair.

Returning from the harbour, Mr Platten learned that his staff had all moved to the American Embassy, to await flights back to the

US. Of course, Mr Platten himself made haste to join them, but for some reason his US citizenship was not exactly recognized by the embassy staff. An apologetic aide offered Mr Platten a voucher for a few nights in an hotel, but Mr Platten turned the offer down.

He returned to his office, where he spent the next three days living off the emergency supplies. His office was like a fortress, and Mr Platten was safe within it.

Two days after the end of the Harrier theft, the El Libertadorense army staged a bloodless coup, and a new junta was installed in the part of the presidential palace that had escaped damage. This new junta declared itself to be temporary, promised free elections by the end of the following year, made public their recognition of the Republic of Delmira, extended reconciliatory wishes to the brave people of Great Britain, and above all declared a major slum-clearance programme for Prudencia.

The bulldozers moved in on Mr Platten's street that same afternoon.

Photoset, printed and bound in Great Britain by REDWOOD BURN LIMITED, Trowbridge, Wiltshire